Bruges-la-Morte

GEORGES RODENBACH

Bruges-la-Morte

TRANSLATED BY WILL STONE

WAKEFIELD PRESS, CAMBRIDGE, MASSACHUSETTS

Wakefield Press, P.O. Box 425645, Cambridge, MA 02142
Originally published in French as *Bruges-la-Morte* (Paris: Ernest Flammarion, 1892). Halftone engravings by Ch.-G Petot and Co., based on the photographs of the Lévy and Neurdein printing house. Frontispiece by Fernand Khnopff.

This book was set in Garamond Premier Pro and Helvetica Neue Pro by Wakefield Press. Printed and bound by McNaughton & Gunn, Inc., in the United States of America.

ISBN: 978-1-939663-81-8

Available through D.A.P./Distributed Art Publishers
75 Broad Street, Suite 630
New York, New York 10004
Tel: (212) 627-1999
Fax: (212) 627-9484

10 9 8 7 6 5 4 3 2 1

TRANSLATOR'S INTRODUCTION

Georges Rodenbach (1855–1898) was born in Tournai, Belgium, but spent his early years in the Flemish city of Ghent where, like his famous compatriots, the writer Maurice Maeterlinck and the poet Émile Verhaeren, he studied law. Having graduated with distinction, Rodenbach duly entered the profession and apparently acquitted himself admirably, but soon the lure of literature was all consuming. Rodenbach was the first Flemish-born French-speaking Belgian symbolist-era writer (a species disparagingly dubbed by emerging Flemish nationalists as "Fransquillons," i.e., French-loving traitors) to install himself in Paris, where he rubbed shoulders with all the main players of the circle around Mallarmé. From 1888, Rodenbach was fully established in the French capital: he rented a swish apartment with his wife Anna and wrote articles for the prestigious newspaper *Le Figaro*. However, despite never having lived there, Rodenbach's name is forever associated with the ancient city of Bruges in West Flanders, the location for his most celebrated and enduring work, the poetically imbued 1892 novel *Bruges-la-Morte*. It is the single work for which Rodenbach is best known, and it has spawned a number of films of variable quality, as well as the opera by Erich Wolfgang Korngold, *Die tote Stadt*, first performed in December 1920. Rodenbach also wrote a series of currently neglected collections of poetry; one of which, *Le Règne du silence* (The reign of silence, 1891), appears through specific poetic imagery and equally melancholy strains to prefigure the now internationally celebrated *Bruges-la-Morte*. A later novel, *Le Carilloneur* (translated as *The Bells of Bruges*, 1897), is also set in Bruges and is concerned with the encroachment of commerce and tourism on the city—what Rodenbach perceived to be the erosion of the fragile "artistic" atmosphere of this preeminent *ville morte*. Further collections of short stories, prose poems, and a range of critical essays on contemporaries such as Rodin, Monet, Huysmans, Verlaine, and Mallarmé attest to a prodigious literary talent. In one sense Rodenbach was a typical artist of the decadent period, unfailingly antibourgeois, solitary, an aesthete suffering some undisclosed malady of the spirit, the victim of a palpable sense of ennui or "spleen." But he was no mere posturing dandy indulging in symbolist embroidered verbosity, a spokesman of his time only and none beyond, but rather, a poet of the first rank, whose legacy outstrips the literary datedness of many of his peers. Like his better-known prose, his morbidly borne, poignant, delicate, yet deceptively existentially muscular poems still offer much to the modern reader. It is interesting to note that in 2020 the Musée d'Orsay in Paris selected a poem by Rodenbach to decorate the catalog of their exhibition on the Belgian artist Léon Spilliaert.

A cloak of melancholy and Thanatos has enveloped the name of Georges Rodenbach like that of no other European poet of the late nineteenth century. Why is this? Like the artist Edvard Munch, who was born only eight years after him, Rodenbach was surrounded by death from an early age owing to a plethora of mortalities in his family. The young Rodenbach was immersed in sickness and death, the raw reality of loss, and this sensitive being struggled lifelong to absorb its terrible significance. He himself would die prematurely from a tubercular lung disease at the early age of forty-three in December 1898, to be buried in an elaborate tomb in Père Lachaise Cemetery that would come to be known as "l'Homme à la Rose." A prose piece dating from 1895 entitled "Les Tombeaux" (The graves) is typical of Rodenbach's interiorized style:

> In this disorder of vegetation, the gravestones loom up, unyielding, geometric. Nothing could disturb them. Even the winds of the October storms are powerless, as if merely pounding on the door of eternity. The sun alone thwarted their impassiveness; as, in spite of them, their shadows transmuted, moving around them. According to the sun's position the grave was now in shadow and now in sunlight. Interlude of light and dark! A pall of darkness over the grave then suddenly a flood of golden light! As if death had in turn opened and closed its eyes.

In Rodenbach's works, the shadow, the breath of death is always present, but its eternal dominion is enclosed in silence, which is sacred. Rodenbach mentions often the "wounding" of silence by voices, by the sound of machines, even by a cough. This silence dwells in inanimate objects, which, though appearing not to be living, in fact secretly hold some greater significance than their plastic reality might suggest. But there exists, too, a silence of places where the activity of reality and human labor has stalled, gradually giving way to decay, to death, most evidently in the labyrinthine canals and lanes of Bruges that figure obsessively in both poetry and prose. For Rodenbach, Bruges is not only a divine repository of the past but a living entity with a personality, a being infused with maturing spiritual and artistic meaning informed by its abandonment and decrepitude, by its extinction. For Rodenbach, Bruges's demise as a thriving port in medieval times owing to the silting up of the Zwijn, which connected the city to the North Sea, meant it could become something altogether at odds with its original function, a city of stasis, a landscape where functional reality found no foothold. The inhabitants' wish for Bruges the dead to become once more Bruges the living again was anathema to Rodenbach.

Today Rodenbach is shunned from any civic remembrance owing to his wish to hold Bruges back from progress, and to his "French treachery." Instead, the nationalist-leaning Flemish religious poet Guido Gezelle takes center stage in the city's monuments. But ironically it was Rodenbach who in some sense restored Bruges to the public's attention with *Bruges-la-Morte*, a text which became the essential literary "guide" to the city for cultured Parisians of the 1890s. This growth in touristic interest evolved over the next century into the mass tourist phenomenon of today, where the city's whole raison d'être is to serve the visitor all year round and canny burghers ensure the ringing of the chocolate shop tills drowns out the carillon. Rodenbach's writings seem to have found their way into the consciousness of both Proust and Rilke, the latter appearing to echo Rodenbach's preoccupation with silence and the hidden life behind objects in works such as the *New Poems* (1907–1908) and *The Notebooks of Malte Laurids Brigge* (1910). In 1906, Rilke made a prolonged sojourn to Furnes and Bruges on the recommendation of Verhaeren, now himself sequestered in Paris. It was the poetry and prose of Rodenbach that Verhaeren urged Rilke to read in preparation for his journey.

Bruges-la-Morte concerns the fate of Hugues Viane, a widower who has turned to the stilled, melancholy atmosphere of Bruges as the ideal location in which to mourn his beloved wife and as a suitable haven for the narcissistic perambulations of his inexorably disturbed spirit. Dead Bruges melds with the image of his dead wife and thus allows Viane to endure the unbearable loss and the resulting existential torment by becoming a protective enclosure. Viane's life plays out at a leisurely, repetitive, almost somnolent pace as he systematically follows the confusing web of streets and canals in a cyclical promenade of reflection and allusion. The story upon which the poetic evocations of Bruges are draped centers around Hugues's obsession with a young dancer of lower status whom he comes to believe through a nervous hallucinated state is the double of his lost wife. Ultimately, though, *Bruges-la-Morte* is a visionary prose meditation on the indefinable aura of Bruges that uses the action of a novel to usher in the images. The story feels secondary to the landscape in which it is played out.

Besides *Le Règne du silence*, another prefiguring text for *Bruges-la-Morte* is "The Death Throes of Towns," an essay written in 1889 but not published until 1897 and thereafter anthologized. This feels like a blueprint for the novel in terms of its Bruges-related themes. Rodenbach leads the reader to the "cemetery" of dead towns in old Flanders, Courtrai, Audenaarde, Furnes, "those melancholic widows of medieval Communes," whose undisputed queen is Bruges. Rodenbach's morbid sensibility is poised to poetically address the atmosphere of the ecclesiastical center basking drowsily in its faded glories. An inviolable silence above all and the "mutedness of color" seem to saturate the city, which, despite its once bustling life, religious pageants, and scrupulously tended piety epitomized by the Beguinage, seems fatefully locked in a decline that uniquely offers aesthetic and spiritual significance.

The photographs, which depict streets, monuments, and select views of the city as it appeared in Rodenbach's day, are one of the most important aspects of *Bruges-la-Morte*. Rodenbach saw these as crucial to the story, and he interspersed them throughout the text, as he explains in his prefatory note, "so our readers will also be subject to the presence and influence of the City, feel the contagion of the neighboring waters, sense in their turn the shadow of the high towers reaching across the text." These photographs are similar to the old postcard views of Bruges one can sometimes find today in souvenir shops. Rodenbach selected them for the book from a firm of commercial photographers. They were intended to display locations, views, monuments, and buildings that served to indicate the imaginative material of the novel. These anodyne, rather perfunctory images are not in themselves artistic; they do not act as pictorial rivals to the text, but serve as breaks, breathing spaces, windows onto the landscape of the writing where the city's landmarks stand as proof that this city is a physical entity that, though emptied of human life, exists, or rather exists in a void before it shall live again. Walter Benjamin's remarks on Atget's photographs could just as well apply here: "Remarkably, however, almost all these pictures are empty. [. . .] They are not lonely, merely without mood; the city in these pictures looks cleared out, like a lodging that has not yet found a new tenant."[1] Rodenbach's use of photographs interspersed throughout the text was groundbreaking, a practice employed thirty years later in *Najda* by André Breton, and in our own time most persuasively and creatively in the works of the author W. G. Sebald.

NOTE

1. Walter Benjamin, *Selected Writings, Volume 2: 1927–1934*, trans. Edmund Jephcott and Kingsley Shorter (Cambridge, MA: Harvard University Press, 1999), 519.

Bruges-la-Morte

PREFACE

~~~~~~~~~~~~~~~

In this study of passion, we wished first and foremost to also evoke a City, the City as principal character, associated with states of the soul, which counsels, dissuades, and induces one to act.

In reality, this Bruges that we have seen to elect appears almost human ... It exerts an influence over those who stay there.

It molds them according to its monuments and its bells.

What we seek to suggest is this: the City directing the action; its urban landscapes no longer mere backdrops, somewhat arbitrarily chosen descriptive themes, but linked to the very events of the book.

And this is why, since these scenes of Bruges impinge upon the story, it is vital to reproduce them here interspersed between the pages: quays, deserted streets, old houses, canals, beguinages, churches, silversmiths offering liturgical wares, belfries, so our readers will also be subject

3

to the presence and influence of the City, feel the contagion of the neighboring waters, sense in their turn the shadow of the high towers reaching across the text.

BRUGES-LA-MORTE

I

Day was fading, darkening the corridors of the large silent house, fitting screens of crepe to the windows.

Hugues Viane was preparing to go out, as was his custom toward late afternoon. Solitary and with little to occupy his time, he would spend the whole day in his large room on the second floor, whose windows gave onto the Quai du Rosaire along which his house extended, mirrored in the water.

He read a little—reviews, old books—smoked much, and daydreamed at the window open to the gray weather, lost in his memories.

For five years now he had lived this way, five years since he had relocated to Bruges in the days following his wife's death. Already five years! And he said to himself over and over: "Widowed . . . to be widowed . . . I am widowed!" A blunt and irremediable word, a single word without an echo. An odd word which well describes the unpaired object.

The separation had been wretched for him: he had known love, in luxury, leisure, travel, and ever-fresh destinations serving to revive the idyll. Not only the tranquil delight of an exemplary conjugal life, but passion undimmed, a fever sustained, kisses barely less intense, the harmony of souls, distant and yet united, like the parallel quays of a canal, which merges their two reflections.

A decade of such joyfulness scarcely felt, so swiftly had time passed!

Then the young woman was gone, on the eve of her thirties, over a matter of weeks she had taken to her bed, so quickly become her deathbed, the image of which he would never forget: faded and white as the candle lighting her, the one he had adored, so beautiful that blossom complexion, her eyes of black dilated pupil, set in mother-of-pearl, the darkness of which contrasted with her hair of an amber yellow, which, loosened, covered her

entire back. The Virgins of the Primitives possess such fleeces which descend with the same hushed quivering.

Hugues had cut away this sheaf from the recumbent corpse, braided into a long plait during the last days of her illness. Is this not death's merciful act? It destroys all but leaves the hair intact. Eyes, lips, all clouds over and falls apart. But the hair doesn't even give up its color. It is in that alone we endure. And now, after five years already, the preserved braid had barely faded, despite the salt of so many tears.

On that day the widower relived his past more painfully, owing to the gray November weather, when it seems the bells are sowing the air with the dust of sound, dead ashes of the years.

And yet he resolved to go out, not to seek outside some inevitable distraction or remedy for his sickness, but because he loved to walk as evening approached and seek analogies to his mourning in the solitary canals and ecclesiastical quarters.

Descending to the first floor, he noticed doors normally kept fastened were all swung wide onto the great white passageway.

In the silence he called to his old servant, "Barbe . . . Barbe! . . ."

Directly the woman appeared in the door frame and, guessing why her master had hailed her, said:

"Monsieur, I had to tidy the drawing rooms today as tomorrow is a Saints Day."

"What Saints Day?" asked Hugues with an air of vexation.

"What, you are not aware, Sir? It's the feast of the Presentation of the Virgin. I must attend Mass and then the service at the Beguinage. It's like a Sunday. And since I cannot work tomorrow, I've tidied the living rooms today."

Hugues Viane did not conceal his displeasure. She knew well enough how he wished to be present when such work was underway. In these two rooms there were too many treasures, too many memories of Her and of the past to let the servant busy herself there on her own. He wanted to keep a weather eye on her, check her movements, monitor her mindfulness, spy on her signs of respect. And when they had to be disturbed for the purposes of dusting, those precious trinkets, a cushion, a screen she had created herself, then he alone wished to be the one to handle them. It was as if her fingerprints still covered this untrammeled and unchanging furniture, sofas, divans, armchairs where she had sat, and which retained, so to speak, the impress of her body. The curtains still displayed the eternal folds she had given them. And the mirrors, it was as if their surfaces should be brushed with sponge or cloth, and with utmost caution so as not to efface her sleeping countenance deep within. But Hugues also wanted to keep watch over and safeguard the portraits of the poor dead woman, portraits made at

different stages of her life and scattered all over, on the mantelpiece, the pedestal tables, the walls; and above all—any misfortune befalling that would have cloven his soul in two—the preserved treasure of the sheaf of hair which he could not bear to lock away in some chest of drawers or gloomy trunk—that would have been like consigning it to the tomb, no, since it was still living and of an ageless gold, better to leave it unfurled on display, like an immortal fragment of his love!

To ensure he could gaze on it unceasingly, this hair which was still *Her*, he had placed it on the long silent piano in the large undisturbed drawing room, recumbent, lifeless: the severed braid, broken chain, rope salvaged from the shipwreck! And to protect it from contamination, from the damp atmosphere which might have discolored it or caused oxidization, he had the idea, naïve if it hadn't been so touching, of keeping it beneath glass, a transparent casket, a crystal box in which that bare braid might repose, so that he could venerate it every day.

For him, as for the silent objects that existed around him, this braid of hair seemed bound to their very being and had evolved into the soul of the house.

Barbe, the old Flemish servant, a bit sullen but devoted and meticulous, knew the precautions necessary regarding these sacred objects, and always approached them with trembling deference. Not very communicative, in black dress and white tulle bonnet, she had the look of a convent nun, and she would often visit the

Beguinage to see Sister Rosalie, her sole relative, who was a beguine.

By frequenting the Beguinage with its pious customs, she had retained that air of silence and gliding tread common to those more accustomed to the flagstones of a church. For this and the fact that she did not surround his grief with noise or laughter, Hugues Viane had found her ideally suited to his needs ever since his arrival in Bruges. He had no other servant and she had become indispensable, despite her innocent tyranny, her sanctimonious old maid habits, and her resolve to do things after her own fashion, as today for example when because of a trivial Saints Day tomorrow, she had turned the living rooms upside down without his knowledge and contrary to his firm instructions.

Before departing Hugues waited for her to reposition the furniture, assuring himself that all he cherished was undefiled and returned to its rightful place. Then, reassured, the doors and shutters fastened, he set out on his usual twilight stroll, despite the unrelenting drizzle, so common in late autumn, a fine vertical rain that wept, weaving the water, threading the air, leaving the still surface of the canal bristling with needles, entrapping and transfixing the soul like a bird in the interminable mesh of a watery net!

~~~~~~~~~~~~~~

RODENBACH

II

Each evening Hugues retraced the same route, following the lines of the quays with hesitant step, already rather stooped although he was only forty. Bereavement had brought an early autumn to his life. His hair receded from the temples and was already peppered with gray ash. His faded eyes searched the distance, the far distance, beyond life.

And how melancholic Bruges was on those late afternoons. And how he loved it just so. It was the melancholy atmosphere which had drawn him here after the great catastrophe. Long ago, in those carefree times when he traveled with his wife, indulging his every fancy, a cosmopolitan existence, Paris, the coastal resorts or foreign shores, they had also come to Bruges whose profound melancholy had been incapable of dulling their rapture. But much later, alone, he recalled Bruges and felt an immediate, intuitive need to settle there. A mysterious equation was forming. The dead city would now correspond to the dead wife. His deep mourning demanded such a setting. Only here would life be bearable. It was instinct alone which had led him there. Beyond, the world could seethe and bustle, light up with festivities and weave its myriad sounds. All he craved was eternal silence and an existence so monotonous he would barely experience the very sensation of being alive ...

Why must one keep silent around physical suffering? Why tread so softly in the sickroom? Why do noises and voices seem to disturb the dressing and reopen the wound?

To moral suffering, noise too can be wounding.

In the stilled atmosphere of the canals and lifeless streets, Hugues was less aware of his heart's suffering and he could reflect more calmly on his dead wife. He could see her, hear her more clearly, and along the canals rediscover her Ophelia face drifting past, hearkening to her voice in the thin and distant song of the carillon.

The city too, once beautiful and beloved, seemed an incarnation of his sense of loss. Bruges was his dead wife. And his dead wife was Bruges. Both were united in a single destiny. This was *Bruges-la-Morte*, she herself entombed in her stone quays, the cold arteries of her canals, where the great pulse of the ocean had ceased to beat.

That evening as he wandered aimlessly, the dark memory haunted him more than ever, emerging from beneath bridges where stone faces weep from invisible

springs. The shuttered houses gave a funereal impression, their windows like eyes clouded in the throes of death, their gables tracing stairways of crepe in the water. He passed alongside the Quai Vert, the Quai du Miroir, beyond the Pont du Moulin, into the mournful suburbs fringed with poplars. And everywhere the cold droplets, the tiny salt notes of the parish bells alighted on his head, as if flicked from an aspergillum during absolution.

In this solitude of evening and autumn when the wind whisked away the last leaves, he felt more than ever a desire to have done with life and an impatience for the tomb. It seemed as if a shadow from the towers stretched over his soul; as if the ancient walls lent him their counsel; as if a whispering voice rose from the water—water coming to him as it had come for Ophelia, as tell Shakespeare's gravediggers.

More than once he had felt thus encompassed. He had heard the slow persuasion of the stones and had truly surprised *the order of things* by not surviving the death all around.

He had imagined killing himself, pondered it deeply and for a long time. Ah, that woman, how he had adored her. Her eyes still upon him! And her voice he still pursued, fled to the furthest horizon! What did she possess, this woman, to make him so utterly besotted, to have deprived him of an entire world from the moment she departed? But there are loves like the Dead Sea fruit that only leaves on the mouth a lingering tang of ash.

If he had resisted the urge to end his life, then that too was for her. The backdrop of his religious childhood had risen in him again with the lees of his suffering. Mystical by nature, he hoped nothingness was not the conclusion to earthly existence and that one day he would see her again. Religious faith protected him from suicide. Such an act would expel him from the bosom of the Lord and extinguish the tentative hope of seeing her again.

And in this way, he lived on; he even prayed, finding reassurance in the image of their future encounter in some heavenly garden; by dreaming of her in the churches, in the swell of the organ's sound.

That evening he passed by Notre Dame, which he often visited to savor its mortuary atmosphere. Everywhere, set in the walls and in the ground, were tomb slabs with skulls, their indented names and worn inscriptions too like lips of stone . . . here was death itself effaced by death . . .

Yet, right beside them, the nothingness of life was illuminated by the consoling vision of love made eternal through death. It was this that drew Hugues on his frequent pilgrimages to the church: the famous tombs of Charles the Bold and Mary of Burgundy at one end of a side chapel. How touching they were! The gentle princess above all, palms clasped together in prayer, head resting on a cushion, attired in a gown of brass, her feet resting on a dog symbolizing fidelity, rigid she lay upon

the slab of the sarcophagus, just as his wife rested eternally on his dark soul. And the time would surely come when he too would rest beside her, like Duke Charles. If they were not to be reunited in the fulfillment of the Christian hope then at least they would sleep side by side, secure in the sanctuary of death.

Hugues left Notre Dame feeling more melancholic than ever. He headed for home, since the hour when he customarily returned for his evening meal was fast approaching. He searched within himself for the memory of his dead wife so he could apply it to the form of the tomb he had just witnessed, and to imagine it with another's face. But the countenance of the dead, preserved in our memories for a time, begins to fade, then gradually wastes away, like a pastel without the protection of glass whose chalk gradually vanishes. And so, within us, our dead die a second time!

While he attempted to recompose her already half-effaced features—as if searching deep within himself— Hugues, who ordinarily scarcely heeded passersby, few as they were, suffered a jolt on seeing a young woman coming toward him. He hadn't even noticed her at first, approaching from the end of the street; it was only when she had drawn near.

At the sight of her, he pulled up short, as if rooted to the spot; the person who was coming in the other direction had passed close by him. This was a shock, an apparition. Hugues seemed to reel for a moment. He covered his eyes with his hands as if dismissing a dream. Then, after a moment's hesitation, he turned to the stranger who was moving away at a slow rhythmic pace. He made an about turn, abandoning the quay he had been following to set off after her. He had to walk quickly to catch up, darting from one pavement to the other, and drawing closer presented a look of such insistence it would have appeared ill-mannered had it not appeared so distraught. The young woman carried on, seeing without looking. Hugues appeared more and more strange and haunted. He had followed her now for several minutes from street to street, drawing closer as if for a decisive inspection, then retreating with a look of fright when it seemed he was getting too close. He appeared both attracted and terrified at once, as by the well in which one seeks to determine a face . . .

So, yes! This time he had surely recognized her, it was undeniable. That pastel complexion, those eyes with their dark dilated pupils set in mother of pearl, they were the very same. And as he walked behind her, that hair which emerged from the nape, beneath the black bonnet and veil, was evidently the selfsame gold, color of amber and silk, a fluid and textured yellow. The same conflict between those nocturnal eyes and the flaming noon of hair.

Had he taken leave of his senses? Or had his retina, in its labor to save the image of his dead wife, identified a passerby with her? While in his mind he sought her face, this woman had suddenly appeared out of the blue to offer him an all-too-perfect replica. How unsettling such an apparition! A miracle of resemblance which steered far too horrifyingly close to being indistinguishable.

And all of it: her walk, her size, the rhythm of her body, the expression of her features, the inward dream of her gaze, it was not only a question of contours and shades, but the spirituality of the being and movement of the soul—all was restored, had reappeared, was alive!

With the air of a sleepwalker, Hugues continued to follow her, but mechanically now, without knowing why, without pause for reflection, through the misty labyrinth of Bruges's streets. Reaching a crossroads that offered a tangle of different routes, and some distance behind, Hugues suddenly lost her from sight. She had vanished down who knew which of those winding side streets.

He stopped, searching the distance, scanning the emptiness, tears welling up in his eyes . . .

Oh, how she resembled his dead wife!

~~~~~~~~~~~~~~

III

The encounter threw Hugues into a state of turmoil. Now when he dreamed of his wife, he saw only this stranger from the other evening; she was her living memory, nothing less. She bore the perfect likeness to his dead wife.

When he went in silent devotion to kiss the relic of preserved hair, or stood deeply moved before her portrait, he no longer confronted the dead woman's image but instead that of the living woman who resembled her. The uncanny equivalence of those two faces. It was as if a fateful mercy had been shown him and furnished his memory with a series of landmarks which connived with him against forgetting, substituting a fresh print for one which was fading, already yellowed and spotted by time.

Hugues now guarded a fresh and untainted vision of his vanished wife. He had only to reach for the memory of the old quay as evening fell that day and a woman approaching him with the face of his dead wife. He no longer had to look backward into the distant years past; it sufficed to dream of the evening before or the one before that. Everything seemed that much closer and clearer now. His eye had once more stored up that beloved face; the recent impression had fused with the old, each reinforcing the other in a resemblance which now almost gave the illusion of a real presence.

In the days that followed, Hugues was a haunted man. So, there was a woman who was an exact double of the one lost. When he saw her pass by him, he had for an instant endured the cruel dream that she would return, had already returned and was coming to meet him as in the past. The same eyes, the same complexion, the same hair—all so alike and right, such a strange caprice of nature and of fate!

He would have liked to see her again. Perhaps he never would. Still, just knowing she was near and that he might meet her made him feel a little less lonely and widowed. Is a man really a widower when his wife is only absent, and makes brief reappearances?

He would imagine he had found his wife again when encountering the woman who resembled her. With this hope he would go at the same hour each evening, to the places where he had seen her. He paced the old quay with its blackened gables, where behind windows framed in muslin like the faces of beguines, idle women, suddenly curious about his comings and goings, peered

at him closely; he slipped down dead streets and meandering alleyways, hoping she might suddenly emerge at the corner of some crossroads.

A week passed in this fashion, in expectation unrewarded. Hugues was already losing hope when, one Monday—the same day as the first encounter—he saw her again, immediately recognizing her as she approached with the same swaying walk. Even more than on the previous occasion she seemed to him a perfect resemblance, consummate and truly terrifying.

From anxious excitement, his heart skipped a beat, as if he might die; blood sang in his ears while visions clouded his eyes: white muslin, wedding veils, communicants in procession. Then, dark and very near now, the mark of her silhouette that would brush against him.

Clearly the woman had noted his air of disquiet, since she regarded him with an air of surprise. Oh, that look recovered, out of the void! That look he had thought never to see again—that he imagined dissolving into the earth—that look was now upon him, fixed and gentle, blossoming again, caressing him anew. A look coming out of the far distance, risen from the tomb, like that which Lazarus must have had for Christ.

Hugues found himself lacking strength, his whole being drawn in the wake of this apparition. The dead woman was before him, closer, and then moving away again. He had to walk directly behind her, get closer to her, observe her, drink in her rediscovered eyes, rekindle his life in her hair made of light. He must follow her, no arguments, plainly to the farthest reaches of the town and to the end of the world.

He hadn't thought it through, but mechanically, he began to walk behind her again, close now, breathless with fear at losing her again, in this ancient city of circuitous and meandering streets.

Of course, he had never dreamt for one minute of adopting such abnormal behavior: following a woman, never! But it was *his* wife he was following, whom he was accompanying on this twilight walk, and would lead back to her tomb . . .

Magnetized, as if in a dream, Hugues walked to one side or just behind the stranger, unaware that they had now left the lonely quay and reached the commercial quarter at the city center, the Grand Place where the towering and somber Tour des Halles warded off the invading night with the gold shield of its clock face.

Slender and swift, the young woman appeared to evade this pursuit and entered the rue Flamande—with its ancient carved, ornamented facades recalling the deck of a ship—emerging in an ever-sharper silhouette each time she passed before the bright shop windows or the spreading glow of a streetlamp.

Then he saw her suddenly cross the street and make her way to the theater whose doors were open, and there she entered.

Hugues did not stop ... He had become a passive will, a satellite drawn in the wake of this apparition. The motion of the soul gathers its own momentum. Yielding to his former impulsion, he in turn entered the foyer where a crowd was converging. But the vision had vanished. The young woman was nowhere to be seen, not amongst the public queuing for tickets, not at the auditorium entrance, nor on the stairways. Where had she disappeared to? Down which corridor? Through which side door? There was no mistake, he had seen her go in. No doubt she was going to see the performance. She would soon be in the auditorium. Maybe she had already taken her seat or was comfortably installed in the crimson darkness of a box. He must find her, see her again, observe her without interruption for a whole evening! He felt his mind fairly quiver at this thought which brought at once a feeling of well-being and discomfiture. But to resist such a notion did not even occur to him. And without pausing to further reflect, neither on the confused bearing he had assumed for the last hour, nor on the folly of his new plan, nor on the anomaly of his attendance at a theatrical performance despite the voluminous cloak of mourning in which he was perpetually attired, he headed without hesitation to the box office, paid for a seat, and entered the auditorium.

His eye quickly scanned the seats, the rows of stalls, the ground floor boxes, those higher up, the upper circle, which were gradually filling up, illuminated by the contagious light of the chandeliers. He couldn't find her, he felt disconcerted, troubled, crestfallen. What evil fate was toying with him? Hallucinatory face revealed then at once concealed! Intermittent apparitions like the moon appearing through clouds! He waited awhile and cast around again. A few latecomers hurried in, finding their places in a creaking of doors and seats.

She alone did not arrive.

He began to regret his heedless action. All the more so seeing he had been noticed and people's astonishment was being directed through their opera glasses, which he was now aware of. To be sure; he kept company with no one, had discouraged contact with members of his own family, and lived alone. In this thinly populated and sleepy city of Bruges, where everyone knew everyone else, inquired after newcomers, and kept each other informed, he was certainly known, at least by sight; they knew who he was and of his noble despair.

It was a surprise, then, practically the end of a legend; and meant victory for those malicious types who had always smiled when people spoke of the inconsolable widower.

Then Hugues became aware, through who knows what effluent emanating from a crowd unified by collective thought, of a personal lapse of judgment, a betrayal of nobleness, a first crack in the vase of his conjugal cult,

from which his sorrow, well tended until now, would drain away completely.

However, the orchestra had just begun the overture of the work being performed. He had read on his neighbor's program the title in large letters, *Robert le Diable*, one of those old-style operas, which almost invariably make up the provincial repertoire. Now the violins were playing the opening bars.

Hugues felt even more perturbed. Since the death of his wife, he had never listened to music. He felt fearful at the song of the instruments. Even an accordion in the streets, with its asthmatic, sour refrain, would have him shedding tears. And likewise the organs, in Notre Dame and Sainte-Walburge on a Sunday, when they seemed to drape black velvet and catafalques of sound over the faithful.

Now the opera music was flooding his brain; the bows played on his nerves. His eyes experienced a tingling sensation. Would he cry again? He thought about leaving when a strange thought crossed his mind: the woman, whom he had pursued as if in a fit of madness and for the balm of her resemblance, was not there, of that he was sure. Yet she had entered the theater virtually before his very eyes. But if she was not to be found in the auditorium, perhaps she was going to appear on stage?

Such profanation tore through his very soul. That same face, his wife's face illuminated in the footlights, overstated by makeup. And if this woman followed until she vanished no doubt through some service door were an actress, was he about to see her suddenly appear gesticulating and singing? Ah! and her voice? Would it be the same voice maintaining that diabolic resemblance—that voice of solemnity, metallic, silver with a hint of bronze—which he had never heard again, ever?

Hugues was shaken at the possibility of following this coincidence to the end; and in a state of anguish, he lingered, with a kind of premonition that his suspicions were justified.

The acts passed, with Hugues none the wiser. He didn't spy her among the singers, nor the chorus, heavily made up and painted like so many wooden dolls. Inattentive to the opera, he had resolved to leave after the scene with the nuns, whose graveyard setting was drawing him back to his morbid introspections. But all of a sudden, during the recitative of the invocation, when the ballerinas, representing convent sisters risen from the dead, process in a long line, when Helena wakening on her tomb and casting off shroud and habit, returns to life, Hugues underwent a shock, like a man emerging from a dark dream who enters a salon where the light flickers in the teetering balance of his eyes.

Yes! it was her! She was a dancer! But he did not muse on that for a moment. This was his dead wife descending the slab of her sepulcher, it was *his* wife who was smiling over there, advancing, holding out her arms.

And more of a resemblance now, a resemblance as to make him weep, with those eyes whose bister only intensified the gloaming, with that hair so present and of a unique gold, like the other . . .

A striking appearance, utterly fleeting, on which the curtain soon fell.

Hugues, his mind aflame, unstrung and glowing, made his way home along the quays, as if again hallucinating from the persistent vision which still opened before him, even in darkest night, its frame of light . . . like relentless Faust after the magic mirror in which the heavenly image of woman is revealed!

~~~~~~~~~~~~~~~~~

IV

Hugues wasted no time finding out about her. He learned her name: Jane Scott, who had star billing on the posters; she lived in Lille and came twice a week with her company to give performances in Bruges.

Dancers are hardly known for being puritans. So, one evening, impelled to get closer to her, seduced as he was by the sorrowful charm of that resemblance, he made his move.

She responded as if expecting the encounter, without the slightest air of surprise and in a voice which moved Hugues to his very soul. The voice too was that of his wife, a perfect replica, a voice of identical timbre, wrought in the very same silver. How the demon of analogy toyed with him! Could there exist, then, a secret harmony in faces, and could the voice perfectly correspond to a particular pair of eyes or head of hair?

And since she possessed those same dark widening pupils set in mother of pearl and that hair of a rare gold and an unobtainable alloy, why wouldn't she have the same manner of speech as the dead woman? Seeing her now more clearly, close up, he could detect no difference between this woman and his dead wife. Hugues remained unsettled by this and the fact that despite her powders, her makeup, and the blaze of the footlights, the woman still had the same perfect natural complexion. And in her look too was none of that casual manner common to dancers: she was soberly dressed, and her conduct seemed gentle and reserved.

Hugues saw her again on a number of occasions and engaged her in conversation. The spell of resemblance was taking hold . . . He had no wish to revisit the theater. That first evening had been a pleasurable trick of fate. Since she had been the illusion of his rediscovered wife, it was only right that she had appeared to him as one raised from the dead, descending from the tomb amidst an extravagant scenery bathed in moonlight.

However, from this point on he stopped imagining her as such. She was the dead wife transformed into living woman, renewing her life in the shadows, dressed in quiet spoken garments. To underpin the illusion, Hugues only wanted the dancer to dress in line with her resemblance.

Now he would often go to visit her each time she was in town, waiting for her at the hotel where she had a room. At first, he was content with the consoling fiction

of her face. There he searched for the dead woman's countenance. For long minutes he would gaze at her in a melancholy rapture, storing up the image of her lips, her hair, her complexion, tracing them all beneath the gaze of his languid eye.... A surge of joy followed as if from the well one thought empty and which now harbors a presence. The water is a void no longer; the mirror lives!

To enhance the illusion of her voice, he would sometimes lower his eyelids while he listened, and he drank in that sound, so identical that one could mistake it for the real thing, save for an instant when it was more muted, a slight muffling around the words, as if the dead woman were speaking from behind a curtain.

And yet of that initial appearance on stage a troublesome memory persisted: he had taken in her bare arms, her throat, the supple line of her back, and now imagined it all filling the empty dress.

A sensual curiosity crept over him.

Who can explain the passionate embrace of a long-separated couple who love each other? Here, death had been merely absence, since the same woman had now resurfaced.

Gazing on Jane, Hugues dreamed of the dead woman, the kisses and embraces of years past. By possessing this woman, he thought to repossess the other. What had seemed over for good would now start afresh. What's more, he wouldn't even be unfaithful to the Spouse, since it was her whom he would love in this effigy, her mouth and hers alone he would kiss.

Hugues experienced a joy both powerful and mournful. He considered his passion righteous rather than a sacrilege, so much had he fused these two women into a single being—lost, rediscovered, forever loved, in the present as in the past, with those matching eyes, indivisible hair, one flesh, a single body to which he would remain devoted.

Now, each time Jane came to Bruges, Hugues would meet her, either in the late afternoon before the performance or more often afterward, in those midnight silences where he sat beside her into the night, enraptured. Despite the evidence, the unremitting pattern of his prodigious mourning, of hotel rooms with their foreign and transitory atmosphere, he gradually convinced himself that the bad times had never been, that it was still his first wife, their home, a loving marriage, that peaceful intimacy before the legally sanctioned embrace.

Those gentle evenings: an enclosed room, inward peace, silence and tranquility, the unity of a couple fulfilled in one another! The eyes, like moths, have forgotten everything. The dark corners, the cold panes, the rain outside, and winter, the bells tolling the death of hours— eyes which flutter about, never venturing beyond the narrow arc of the lamps!

Hugues relived those nights ... utter oblivion! A new beginning! Time flows down a slope, on a bed free of stones ... and it seems as if living, we are already in eternity.

V

Hugues installed Jane in a pleasant house he had rented for her, along a promenade that led into leafy suburbs dotted with windmills.

At the same time, he had induced her to leave the theater behind, so as to keep her in Bruges and more for himself. Not for a moment, though, had he paused to reflect on the absurdity that a man of his age, known for his inconsolable grief, would become infatuated with a dancer. The truth is, he did not love her. All he wanted was to perpetuate the illusion of this mirage. When he took Jane's head in his hands and drew it close to him, it was to look into her eyes, to search there for something he had seen in another's: some nuance, a reflection, pearls, a flora whose root is in the soul—and which maybe were floating there.

At other times, he would untie her hair so it flooded her shoulders, mentally matching it to those absent tresses, as if he could somehow spin them together.

Jane understood none of Hugues's strange behavior or his silent reveries.

She recalled his inexplicable sadness when at the beginning of the relationship she had told him that she dyed her hair. Ever since and with what intensity of emotion had he inquired to ensure she had kept the same shade.

"I don't want to dye it anymore," she declared one day.

He had seemed terrible disturbed by this, insisting that she retained that bright gold he so adored. And as he spoke, he had held her hair and caressed it, sinking his fingers through it, like a miser who has just recovered his treasure.

And he had babbled in a confused manner: "Don't change a thing . . . I love you because you're like this. You cannot know, you'll never know what it's like to feel your hair . . ."

He appeared to want to add something but pulled up short, as if at the edge of an abyss of confidence.

Since her move to Bruges, he came to see her almost every day, usually passing the evening at her house, occasionally dining there, despite his old servant Barbe's bad moods, when the following day she would gripe at having prepared a meal and waited up for him in vain.

Barbe pretended to believe that he had really dined in a restaurant; but deep down remained incredulous and no longer recognized her formerly punctual and home-loving master.

Hugues went out a good deal, dividing his time between Jane's house and his own.

He preferred to call on her toward evening, given his custom of not leaving home until late afternoon, but he had also purposely chosen a deserted corner of town so he would not be so conspicuous on his way to and from her lodgings. He had felt no shame for himself, no abasement. He knew the motives, the stratagem of this transposition was not only an excuse, but absolution and rehabilitation before the dead woman and even before God. But he still had to reckon with the prudishness of the provinces: how could he not be a little anxious about the neighbors, of public hostility or respect, when he constantly felt their eyes following his every move, as if touching him?

And even more so here in this Catholic Bruges where morals are so strict! The lofty towers in their habits of stone cast their shadow over everything. It was as if a mistrust of the hidden rose of the flesh emanated from the innumerable convents, a contagious glorification of chastity. At every street corner, in cases of wood or glass, was the blessed Virgin, adorned in velvet robes, set amidst faded paper flowers, holding in her hand the unfurled banderole which on her side proclaimed: "I am the immaculate one."

Here, lustful passion and extramarital relations are always considered perverse, the road to Hell, the sin of the sixth and ninth commandments which keeps voices lowered in confession and leaves the penitents flushed with confusion.

Hugues knew well this austerity of Bruges and was at pains to avoid causing it offence. But in such a confined provincial setting nothing escapes notice. Without being aware of it, he was soon subjected to pious indignation. Scandalized faith willingly communicates itself in ironic mockery, the way the cathedral laughs and scoffs at the devil through the masks of its gargoyles.

When the affair between the widower and dancer began to do the rounds, Hugues unwittingly became the laughingstock of the town. No one was immune: gossip spread from door to door; idle talk, tittle-tattle, welcomed with that beguine-like inquisitiveness; weeds of scandalmongering, which push up between the cobblestones in the dead cities.

They amused themselves still more when they learned of his drawn-out despair, his monotonous lamentation, all those thoughts gathered one by one and tied in a bouquet destined for a tomb. And so this was where it ended up, that mourning they had imagined eternal.

Everyone had been taken in by it, even the poor widower himself, who had clearly been bewitched by

this strumpet: well, she had something of a reputation. She was a former dancer at the theater. They pointed her out as she went by, laughing, indignant at her unconcerned air which was betrayed by her yellow hair and swaying walk. They even knew where she lived and that the widower visited her each evening. A little more and they would supply exact times and itineraries . . .

In the emptiness of idle afternoons, the ever-curious good ladies of Bruges would watch Hugues pass by, ensconced in their casement windows, spying on him in their little mirrors known as *espions*, which one notices attached to the outer window ledges of every house. Oblique mirrors which frame the questionable profile of the street; tiny mirror traps which unbeknownst to passersby capture their gestures, their smiles, the thought of a moment revealed in their eyes, and reflect all of this back into the interiors of houses where someone keeps watch.

And so, thanks to the treachery of the mirrors, they all too soon knew everything of Hugues's comings and goings and every last detail of the virtual concubinage in which he and Jane now lived. The illusion in which he persisted, his naïve precautions of going out only at dusk, grafted a kind of mockery onto the liaison which had at first offended, but now the indignation had turned into laughter.

Hugues suspected nothing. He continued to set out at dusk, making his way by various meandering routes to the neighboring suburb.

How much less painful for him were these twilight walks now! He crossed the city, the century-old bridges, the mortuary quays along which the water sighs. The evening bells rang for some memorial service the following day. Ah! The pealing of those bells, but receding—it seemed—and already distant, chiming as if in some other sky . . .

And in vain did the overflowing gutters drip, the tunnels of the bridges sweat cold tears, the poplars by the water tremble like the lament of some half-hearted inconsolable spring. Hugues no longer heard the sorrow of things; nor did he see the rigid city swathed in the myriad bandages of its canals.

City of another age, this Bruges-la-Morte, of which he also seemed the widower, only touched him now with the faintest glow of melancholy. Consoled, he walked on through its silence, as if Bruges too had suddenly emerged from its tomb and offered itself as a new city resembling the old.

While he went each evening to find Jane again, he felt not a shred of remorse, not for a moment a sense of betrayal, for the great love collapsed into parody, of the withdrawal from grief—not even that slight shiver which runs through the widow's marrow when for the first time she pins a red rose to her crepe and cashmere.

~~~~~~~~~~~~~~~~

RODENBACH

VI

Hugues reflected: What indefinable power there is in resemblance!

It corresponds to those two contradictory needs in human nature: habit and novelty. Habit, which is the law, the very rhythm of being. Hugues had experienced it so powerfully that surely it must determine his fate. Having lived for ten years alongside a woman so dear to him, he could not let go of the habit, and his mind lingered over the absent one, seeking her face in those of strangers.

On the other hand, the taste for novelty is no less instinctive. One grows weary of possessing the same thing. Like health, one can only truly appreciate contentment through contrast. And love is the same with its intermittent appearance.

Resemblance, then, is what precisely reconciles these two needs within us, drawing an equivalence and unifying them at some indefinite point. Resemblance is the horizon line of habit and novelty.

And even more so in the case of love, this type of refinement has its effect: the charm of a new woman suddenly appearing who perfectly resembles the old!

Hugues relished this with increasing delight; his solitude and grief had long made him sensitive to such nuances of the soul. And moreover, was it not the idea of those alluring analogies that had lured him to Bruges when he became a widower?

He possessed what might be termed "the sense of resemblance," an additional sensory faculty, both sickly and fragile, which made connections by a thousand tenuous threads, even linking the trees to the Blessed Virgin herself, forging an ethereal telegraphy between his soul and the inconsolable towers.

And it was for this he had chosen Bruges, Bruges from which like some great joy the sea had retreated.

That was already a phenomenon of resemblance, and now his thought would be in perfect harmony with the most significant of the Gray Cities.

The melancholy of those gray Bruges streets, where every day seems like All Saints Day! That grayness, as if distilled from the white caps worn by nuns and the black cassocks of priests, which all passed in a never-ending contagious procession. An enigma of grayness, an eternal half-mourning!

Along every street the facades formed an infinitude of shade: some a pale green wash or faded brick repainted in white; but alongside them, others were of a darker hue, an oppressive charcoal, burnt etchings whose inks console and compensate the brighter neighboring tones; but ultimately, it's always that same grayness which surfaces, hovers, and spreads itself along the line of the walls, aligned at the same angle as the quays themselves.

One senses the song of the bells too as rather somber; now muffled and melting in the air, it evolves into an equitable murmuring grayness which is drawn along, rebounding, rippling across the water of the canals.

And this water, despite so many reflections: corners of blue sky, roof tiles, the snow of swans drifting by, the green of poplars lining the quays, all are woven into tracks of colorless silence.

By some miracle of climate, or shared sentience, who knows what atmospheric chemistry neutralizes the more animated shades, assembling them into a unity of dream, an amalgam of gray lethargy.

It was as if the frequent mist, the veiled light of the northern heavens, the granite of the quays, the incessant rain, and the bells passing through had together influenced the very color of the air—and also in this ancient town, the dead embers of time, the dust from the hourglass of the accumulating years, over everything, its silent legacy.

That was the reason Hugues had wished to seek refuge there, to feel his final energies imperceptibly and irrevocably silt up, sucked down beneath this fine dust of eternity which too lent a grayness to his soul, the color of the city.

Now, through this sudden and seemingly miraculous encounter, this sense of resemblance had acted again, but this time in the opposite way. How and by what quirk of fate had that face abruptly loomed up to revive his early memories, in this Bruges now at such a distance from them?

Despite the bizarre coincidence, Hugues now surrendered himself to the intoxication of Jane's resemblance to his dead wife, in the same way he had formerly glorified the resemblance of himself to the city.

~~~~~~~~~~

VII

In the few months since Hugues had encountered Jane, nothing could dispel the falsehood of his new way of life. How everything had been transformed! He was no longer lost to melancholy nor gave the impression of his solitude existing within an immense void. Jane had revived his love of times past, recalled she who had never seemed so distant and out of reach. He was rediscovering his beloved and seeing her just as one sees the moon traced on the water.

And it was so clearly the dead woman whom he continued to venerate in the simulacrum of this resemblance, which he had never imagined for a moment would compromise the fidelity to his cult of memory for her. Each morning, since the day of her death, he had tendered his devotion—as if at stations on the way of love's cross—before the relics preserved in her honor. Immediately on rising he would pass into the silent shadow of the rooms, with blinds half-open and furniture undisturbed, to experience deep emotion before her portraits: here, a photograph of her as a young woman just before their engagement; at the center of a panel, a large pastel whose reflecting frame alternately concealed and revealed her in intermittent silhouette; and there on the pedestal table, another photograph in a pearl inlaid frame, a portrait of later years, where like an inclining lily, she already imparted an air of affliction ... Hugues placed his lips there and kissed them as if they were the most holy of reliquaries.

Each morning he would also contemplate the crystal casket where the dead woman's hair, ever conspicuous, rested. But rarely had he ever lifted the lid. He didn't dare remove it and run those locks through his fingers. For this hair was sacred! It was the only part of her to evade the tomb and sleep on in a more just repose, here in this coffin of glass. But it was dead all the same and was born of death and therefore must not be disturbed. He had to be content with merely gazing on it, knowing it to be whole, reassuring himself it was always present, this hair upon which perhaps the very soul of the house depended.

Hugues then spent many long hours revivifying his memories, while above his head in the enshrouded silence of the rooms, the chandelier's aspergillus of quivering crystal emitted a drizzle of light lament.

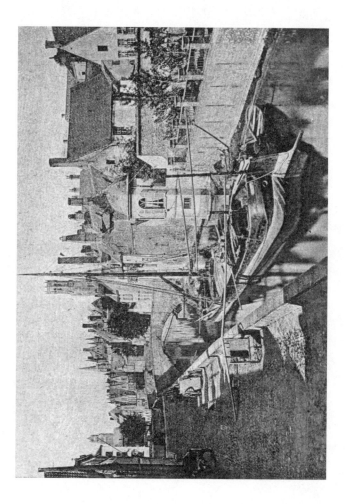

And then he went to Jane as his final station of devotion, Jane who possessed the full living head of hair, Jane who resembled the portrait of his dead wife. One day, trying to delude himself over some particular identification, Hugues had entertained a curious idea, an idea which immediately seduced his entire being: not only would he preserve objects relating to his wife, her trinkets and portraits, but everything that belonged to her, as if she were merely absent. Nothing had been disposed of, given away, or sold off. Her bed chamber was always maintained in readiness for a possible return, all was neat and ordered, with fresh sprigs of boxwood blessed annually. Her untouched linen was neatly arranged in drawers filled with perfumed sachets which preserved them in a somewhat yellowed stillness. The dresses too, all the old garments hung in the wardrobes, silks and poplins drained of movement.

On occasion Hugues wished to see them again, keen to forget nothing and eternalize his sorrow . . .

Love, like faith, is sustained by minor observances. One day a strange desire entered his mind, a notion which would haunt him until its fulfillment: to see Jane in one of those dresses, dressed as the dead woman had been. Such a striking resemblance could only be deepened by adding those garments to the identity of her face, to reaffirm the return of his wife.

What a divine moment it would be when Jane moved toward him dressed like that, a moment which would abolish both time and reality and render his forgetting absolute!

Having penetrated his being, this notion became rooted there, an obsession.

A decision was reached: one morning, he called his old servant and asked her to help him carry a trunk down from the attic which would serve to contain a few of these precious dresses.

"Is Monsieur going on a journey?" asked old Barbe who, unable to account for her habitually reclusive master's new way of life, his departures and sudden absences, his meals out, began to wonder if he had taken leave of his senses.

She helped him bring out the clothes, sort through them, and free them of the clouds of dust which billowed up in those wardrobes so long sunk in stillness.

He chose two dresses, the last his wife had acquired, and laid them out carefully in the trunk, straightening the skirt and smoothing out the creases.

Barbe understood none of this, but it shocked her to see this hitherto undefiled wardrobe being divided up. Were they going to be sold? She ventured:

"What would poor Madame say?"

Hugues looked at her. He had turned pale. Had she guessed? Did she know?

"What are you trying to say?" he demanded.

"I think," replied old Barbe, "that in my village in Flanders, if clothes belonging to the dead have not been sold straightaway during the week of the burial, one is obliged to keep them for the remainder of one's own life, on pain of maintaining the dead in purgatory until one's own passing."

"Don't worry," a relieved Hugues replied. "I have no intention of selling anything. Your tale is indeed quite correct."

But Barbe remained anxious when she saw him a little later, despite all he had just said, load the trunk onto a carriage and depart.

Hugues had no idea how to broach this bizarre scheme to Jane; since out of a sense of delicacy or modesty with regard to the dead woman, he had never spoken to her of his past, nor even alluded to the divine and cruel resemblance which shadowed her.

The trunk set down before her, Jane let out cries of pleasure and leapt about: what a surprise! He had filled it to the brim no doubt, but with what? Gifts? A dress?...

"Yes, dresses," affirmed Hugues mechanically.

"Oh, you are so very kind! And there's more than one?"

"Two."

"What color? Quick, let me see!"

And she advanced toward him, hand outstretched, demanding the key.

Hugues was tongue-tied. He dared not speak, not wanting to betray himself and be obliged to explain the impulsive and pathological desire to which he had yielded.

The trunk flung open, Jane quickly drew out the dresses and looked them over with a quick glance, clearly disappointed:

"What a frumpy style! And this design in silk, how old is that, must be ancient! But where on earth did you buy such dresses? And the cloth of this skirt! Why, that was in vogue a decade ago. I think you must take me for a fool . . ."

Hugues remained bewildered and sheepish; he desperately searched for words, some explanation, not the true one, but one which might seem plausible. He began to see the foolishness of his idea, and yet it still held him in its grip.

Oh, that she might consent! If only she would slip on one of those dresses just for a moment! And this moment when he saw her dressed like his wife, would for him mean the ultimate paroxysm of resemblance and an eternity of forgetting.

He explained to her in a cajoling manner: "Yes, certainly, they were old dresses . . . which he had inherited . . . those of a relative . . . he had just wished to play a little joke . . . had the thought of seeing her in one of these old gowns. It was a crazy idea; but he had wished it all the same . . . if only for a moment!"

Jane understood none of it; she was just laughing, turning each garment over in her hands, assessing the material, a rich silk which had barely faded, but she remained incredulous at this curious and faintly absurd style which nonetheless had once been the epitome of fashion and elegance . . .

Hugues insisted.

"But you'll only think me ugly!"

At first confounded by this caprice, Jane ended up treating the dressing up in these outmoded cast-offs as something of a joke. Giggling childishly, she had slipped out of her robe, with her arms bare, adjusting the bodice which covered her corset, and folding it back along with the lace of her blouse, she slipped into the more low-cut of the two dresses . . . Standing before the mirror, Jane laughed to see herself thus attired: "I look like one of those old portraits!"

And she assumed an affected air, made as if to pirouette; mounted a table and hitched up her skirts to get a better view at how she looked, still laughing, her throat trembling into spasms, one hem of her chemise loosely fastened and revealing the bodice beneath, showing the bare flesh, scarcely chaste and conjuring those intimacies associated with lingerie . . .

Hugues reflected. This moment which he had dreamt of as the epic culmination of resemblance now appeared trivial and cheapened. Jane was relishing the game. Imbued with a wild gaiety she now wanted to try on the other dress, and she began to dance, multiplying her vertical leaps, in a choreography.

Hugues felt a burgeoning sickness of the soul; he had the feeling of being part of a distressing masquerade. For the first time, the distinction of physical resemblance had not sufficed. It had in fact worked, but in the wrong way. Without the resemblance Jane appeared to him merely vulgar. Because of the resemblance, she afforded him, if only for a moment, that terrible impression of seeing his dead wife once more, but now demeaned despite the identical face and dress—the impression one experiences on days of holy processions when in the evening one encounters those who wore the face of the Virgin or one of the female saints, still rigged out in coats or pious tunics, but rather drunk, fallen in with a mystic carnival, beneath streetlamps whose wounds bleed into the shadows.

~~~~~~~~~~~~~~

VIII

One Sunday morning in March, Easter Sunday, old Barbe learned from her master that he would not be taking dinner or supper at home, and that she was free until the evening. She was thrilled with this news since her day off happened to coincide with a major holiday; she would visit the Beguinage and take part in the services—high mass, vespers, the benediction—and would spend the remainder of the day with her relative, Sister Rosalie, who lived in one of the principal convents of the religious enclosure.

Visiting the Beguinage was one of the few genuine pleasures in Barbe's life. Everyone knew her there. She had a number of friends among the beguines and dreamed of her old age, when having amassed some savings, she herself would retreat there, don the veil, and end her life like so many others—so contented!—those whom she would see there with the simple cornet swathing their aged heads of ivory.

Even more so on this youthful March morning, she exalted in heading off to her beloved Béguinage, her voluminous black hooded cloak swaying like a bell. In the distance, the unanimous pealing of parish bells seemed in rhythm with her steps, and among them, every quarter hour, the music rained down, the trembling carillon, like a tune tapped out on a keyboard of glass . . .

The emergence of springtime greenery lent the suburb a rural air. Although Barbe had been resigned to city life for over thirty years, she had retained, like her peers, the undying memory of her village, a peasant soul still inwardly touched by a patch of grass or some leafage.

What a fine morning! And now she quickened her step in the clear sunlight, moved by a bird's cry, the scent of young shoots in this already rustic suburb where corners of greenery joined to form *Minnewater*—the lake of love, as it translates, but better than that: the waters where one loves! And there, before this slumbering pool, the lilies, like the hearts of the first communicants, the grassy banks of massed flowerets, the great trees, the windmills on the horizon, moving, again Barbe experienced the illusion of journeying, of return, over the fields, back to her childhood . . .

She was also a pious soul, from that Flemish faith in which the sediment of Catholic Spain endures, that faith in which scruples and terror rule over belief and

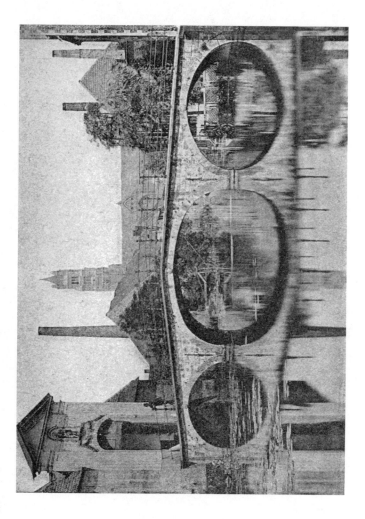

the fear of Hell presides over a yearning for heaven. And yet also with a love of scenery, the sensuality of flowers, of incense, of rich fabrics, which belongs to that race. This is why the arcane soul of the old servant rejoiced in anticipation of the ceremonies to come as she crossed the arched bridge of the Beguinage and passed into its mystic enclosure.

Here, the silence of a church prevailed; even the sound of the delicate springs outside emptying into the lake carried over like the murmur of mouths in prayer; and the enclosing walls, those low walls that trace the convents, white as the tablecloths used for communion. At center a small area of thick lawn, a meadow of Jan Van Eyck, where a lone sheep grazed, suggesting the paschal lamb.

Narrow lanes, bearing the names of saints or the blessed turn sharply, veer off at angles or stretch away, forming a medieval hamlet, a miniature city cloistered within the main one, and even more dead. So empty, so still, with a silence so contagious that one treads softly, speaks in hushed tones, as in the home of one who is ill.

If by chance some passerby approaches and makes a sound, one has the impression of something abnormal and sacrilegious. In this extinct atmosphere only a handful of beguines move about, with soft tread; for they appear to glide rather than walk, like swans, sisters to the white swans of the long canals. A few latecomers hurried beneath the elms on the opposite bank as Barbe headed toward the church where the sound of the organ and the singing of the Mass echoed. She entered with the beguines who went to take their places in the choir, in the double row of sculpted wooden pews. All the white caps sat next to each other, their linen wings rigid, stilled, white with reflections of red and blue traced on them when the sun passed across the stained glass. Barbe looked on with envy from a distance at the kneeling group of sisters, brides of Jesus and servants of God, hoping that perhaps one day she would join them . . .

She had taken her place in one of the side aisles of the church, among a scattering of other dedicated lay persons: elderly men, children, poor families lodged in vacant houses of the Beguinage. Barbe, who had never learned to read, was telling a large rosary, praying fervently, casting the odd glance to one side where her relative Sister Rosalie occupied the second seat in the pews after the Reverend Mother.

How beautiful this church was, all lit up with candles. Barbe, during the offertory, went to purchase a little candle from the sacristan nun who stood beside an iron grille, where soon the old servant's offering was burning in its turn.

From time to time, she followed the slow burning down of her candle, which she could still make out among the others.

How happy she was! And how right of the priests to say that this church is God's house! Especially here at the

Beguinage where the sisters themselves sang in the rood loft with soft voices which could only have been those of angels.

Barbe never tired of listening to the harmonium, and those canticles which unfolded so purely white, like the finest linen.

In the meantime, Mass was said; the lights were being extinguished.

Altogether in a quivering of cornets the beguines made their way out, a swarm which took flight and for a moment spread their white wingspan over the green garden, like a flock of gulls. Barbe followed Sister Rosalie, but at a respectful distance; then, on seeing Rosalie enter her convent, she quickened her pace and a moment later followed her relative inside.

There are several beguines in each of the residencies which make up the community. Three or four here, fifteen or twenty there. Sister Rosalie's was one of the larger communities; and all the sisters just back from church were busy chatting and laughing, questioning each other in the large workroom. Owing to the holiday, baskets of needlework and squares of lace were arranged in the corners. Some of the sisters were in little gardens just in front of the lodgings, poring over plants, checking for growth in the flower beds bordered with boxwood. Others, often the younger ones, were showing off their recent gifts, sugar-frosted Easter eggs. Barbe, somewhat intimidated, followed her relative through the bedrooms and parlors where other visitors had already thronged, fearful of remaining isolated or appearing intrusive, waiting anxiously for an invitation to dine, as was the custom. Oh dear! What if owing to today's influx of visiting relatives there was no place for her at table?

Barbe was reassured when Sister Rosalie came to invite her on behalf of the Reverend Mother, apologized for having neglected her, being caught up elsewhere, for it happened to be her turn among the beguines to direct household duties.

"We'll have a chat after the meal," she added. "Especially as I have something serious to tell you."

"Something serious?" replied Barbe, suddenly worried. "Then tell me right away."

"I don't have time now . . . later . . ."

And she slipped away down the corridor leaving the old servant distraught. Something serious? What could it have to do with her? Some mishap? But she had no one dearer in the world than her sole relative.

Then it must have something to do with herself. But how could she be reproached, of what could she be accused? She had never cheated a soul. When she went to confession, she never knew quite what to say nor which sin she might be guilty of.

Barbe remained in a state of nervousness. Sister Rosalie had given such a grave impression, her tone was almost severe. The joyous day was suddenly at an end. She no longer had the will to laugh or intermingle with the groups who all around were still chattering away and making merry, examining fresh lacework, new patterns to which the inextricable threads from the bobbins were conducted.

Alone, seated to one side, she now pondered over the unknown subject on which Sister Rosalie was about to expound.

After grace had been said they sat down at the table in the long refectory. Barbe picked at her food without any discernible pleasure, while she watched the healthy rosy-faced beguines and other invited relatives like her do justice to this festive Sunday repast. They served wine that day, a wine from Tours, unctuous and golden. Barbe drained the glass she had been served in the hope that it would drown her sorrows. She felt a headache coming on.

The dinner seemed interminable. As soon as it was finally over, she dashed straight to Sister Rosalie with a quizzical look on her face. Rosalie noted her distress and quickly attempted to reassure her.

"It's really nothing, Barbe! Please my dear, don't concern yourself so."

"What is it then?"

"Nothing so serious. A little counsel I must give you."

"Oh, you really worried me . . ."

"When I say nothing serious, I mean at present. But this thing could become much more serious. It's this: it may be advisable for you to find another position."

"Another position, but why? I've been with Monsieur Viane for five years. I am loyal to him because I've seen his unhappiness with my own eyes, and what's more he relies on me. He's the most honorable man in the world."

"Oh, my poor girl, how naïve you are! In fact, no, he is not the most honorable man in the world."

Barbe had turned quite pale and asked:

"What are you trying to say? What has my master done wrong?"

Sister Rosalie then recounted her the story which had spread throughout the town and had even leaked into the sacred enclosure of the Beguinage: the shocking behavior of a widower whom everyone had once admired for his noble and inconsolable grief. Well then! He had consoled himself in the most atrocious fashion! He was now seeing an ex-theater dancer, a woman with something of a dubious reputation . . .

Barbe shuddered as the words sunk in and an inner revulsion welled up; for she revered her relative, and these incredible, highly offensive revelations, so unimaginable to her, carried an authority when they issued from her lips. So that would explain the changes to his routine which had left her so perplexed, the frequent departures, the comings and goings, meals out, returning late at night, nocturnal absences . . . ?

The beguine continued:

"Barbe, have you considered that an honest and Christian servant cannot possibly remain in the service of a man who has turned out to be a libertine?"

At that word Barbe erupted: it was simply not possible! Slander, all of it, and Sister Rosalie had been deceived. Such a decent master, who adored his wife! He who still each morning, before her own eyes, would weep beneath the portraits of the dead woman and treated her hair with the same reverence as one would a holy relic.

"It's just as I tell you," replied Sister Rosalie calmly. "I know everything about it. I even know the house where this woman lives. It's on the street I take into town, and more than once I've seen Monsieur Viane coming and going."

This confirmed it. Barbe appeared crushed. She did not respond, lost in her thoughts, a deep furrow and worry lines showed on her brow.

The she said simply, "I'll give it some thought," while her relative, summoned back to her duties again, left her awhile.

The old servant remained dumbfounded, shaken, her ideas became muddled faced with this news which was so at odds with her principles and threatened the very path of her future.

Firstly, she had an attachment to her master, and it would be a wrench to take leave of him. And then what other post would she find as agreeable, undemanding, and lucrative as this? In that bachelor household she would have been able to gradually build a nice little nest egg with which to end her days at the Beguinage. But Sister Rosalie was right. She could no longer serve a man embroiled in a public scandal.

She was already aware that one cannot remain in service to the impious, those who do not pray or observe the laws of the church. The same reason existed for persons of a debauched nature. They were guilty of the worst of sins, which the preachers warned in their sermons left them easy prey to the devil. And Barbe quickly suppressed any idea of vague culpability in such licentiousness, the very mention of which caused her to ardently cross herself.

How to reach a decision? Barbe remained deeply confused all through vespers and the Solemn Benediction, the celebration of which she returned with the community to the church. She prayed to the Holy Ghost for guidance; and her orisons were granted, when, on leaving the church, she suddenly made her decision.

Since this was a thorny issue and beyond her own powers of judgment, she would proceed without delay to her usual confessor at Notre Dame and obediently follow his counsel.

The priest in whom she confided, who had known this simple soul for years, this soul who ever goaded by scruples which made her dark needy spirit really seem as if crowned by thorns, sought to calm her and made her

promise not to act impetuously: if what they said about her master were true and he was guilty of such liaisons, there was still a case for discrimination on her part, since these encounters had taken place outside the household and she had to put them out of her mind or at least not allow them to trouble her so; and if by some misfortune this woman of ill repute were to visit her masters house, to dine for instance, or for anything else, she could in this case no longer be complicit in such profligacy and should relinquish her service and depart.

Barbe made him repeat this distinction a second time; then, having understood it fully, she left the confessional and made her way from the church after a brief prayer, returning along the Quai du Rosaire to the house she had left in such high spirits that morning and from which she somehow sensed sooner or later she would be forced to depart . . .

Ah, how elusive is enduring happiness! And she returned home by way of the dead streets, nostalgic for the verdurous suburb of that now distant dawn, the Mass, the white canticles, all that on which night was now falling. She pondered looming departures, new faces, her master in a state of mortal sin; and saw herself, with no hope now of ending her days at the Beguinage, dying on an evening like this, quite alone, in the poorhouse whose windows gave onto the canal . . .

IX

Hugues had experienced a profound sense of disillusion-
ment from the day he had entertained that bizarre idea
of dressing Jane in one of his wife's old-fashioned dresses.
He had gone too far. Through wanting to actively con-
join the two women, their resemblance had in fact been
weakened. As long as they remained at a distance from
one another, with the mist of death between them, the
deception was possible. But drawn close together, differ-
ences emerged.

At the beginning, so overwhelmed by the recovery
of that identical face, his emotional state had been complicit; then, gradually, through his desire to break up the
parallels into fragments, he had ended up merely tor-
menting himself over nuances.

Resemblances are never just to be found in the figure, or in an overall impression. If one labors over the
minutiae everything seems different. But unaware that

he himself had altered his way of looking and comparing with ever more meticulous attention to detail, Hugues attributed the fault to Jane and mistakenly believed she herself was totally transformed.

Certainly, she still possessed those same eyes. But if eyes are a window on the soul, surely another soul was emerging from them now, rather than those, ever present, of the dead woman. Jane, gentle, respectful, and reserved at the outset, was now increasingly letting herself go. A lingering odor of the backstage and the auditorium reappeared. Intimacy had encouraged a certain laxity in her appearance and all day long in the house a boisterous and ungainly gaiety reigned, loose chatter, her usual smart outfits seemed disheveled, her hair became unkempt. Hugues's dignified demeanor took offence. Yet he still paid her visits, seeking to recapture the fading mirage. Oh, those gloomy hours! The sullen evenings! He had such a need of that voice. He still drank from its dark stream. And at the same time, he suffered the spoken word.

As for Jane, she was wearying of his dark moods and protracted silences. Now, when he arrived toward evening, she had not yet returned, delayed on some stroll around town, or from shopping and trying on dresses. He also came to see her during the day, both mornings and afternoons. She was often out, tired of staying at home and bored with her lodgings, ever wandering the streets. Where was she off to? Hugues really knew

nothing of her acquaintances. He waited for her. He was ill at ease there alone, preferring to walk about the neighborhood until her return. Dejected, troubled, fearing the searching look, he walked aimlessly, adrift, from one pavement to another, making for the nearest quay, where he walked beside the water. Eventually he would arrive at those symmetrical squares made sad by their trees' lament and from there he slipped into the unfathomable tangle of gray streets.

Ah! Always that grayness in the streets of Bruges!

Hugues felt his soul gradually give in to this gray influence. He submitted to the contagion of the diffuse silence, of this void bereft of passersby. Only a few old women who, like shades in their black cloaks and hooded heads, were returning from lighting a candle in the chapel of the Holy Blood. A curious thing: one never sees as many old women in one place as in these ancient cities. Already the color of the earth, they trudge along aged and unspeaking, as if they had used up all their words . . . Hugues, walking aimlessly, barely noticed them, so absorbed was he in anxieties both old and new. Mechanically he made his way back to Jane's house. But still she had not returned!

He set out again, then hesitated, moving in circles down the decayed streets and ended up back on the Quai du Rosaire. Then he resolved it was time to return home; he would look in on Jane later that evening. Hugues settled into an armchair and tried to read; then, only seconds later, sunk in solitude and encroached on by the cold silence of those long passageways, he went out once more.

Evening . . . it was drizzling, a fine rain which spread and suddenly quickened, pinning his soul . . . Hugues felt himself recaptured, haunted by the face, driven on toward Jane's house; he made his way there and drawing near abruptly retraced his steps, seized by a sudden need for isolation, fearful now that she was there waiting and had no desire to see him.

At a brisk pace he walked in the opposite direction, threading through the old quarters, wandering with no clear direction, in a vague and pitiful manner through the mud. The rain became heavier, spooling its threads, intertwining its cloth, stitches ever tighter, a damp impalpable net in which Hugues gradually felt himself weaken. He began to recollect . . . he thought of Jane. What was she doing at such an hour, outside, in this miserable weather? He thought of the dead woman . . . What, too, had become of her? Oh, her poor grave . . . all the wreathes and flowers ruined from these downpours . . .

And the bells were ringing, so pale, so distant! How far off was the town! It was as if it too no longer existed, was melting away, drowned in the rain that submerged all . . . A matching melancholy! For Bruges-la-Morte alone were those parish bells in the loftiest surviving belfries still falling, sounding their affliction!

X

As Hugues sensed his touching delusion escaping him, so he turned back to the City, connecting its soul with his own, striving for that other parallel with which formerly, when as a widower first arrived in Bruges, he had immersed his grief. Now that Jane was no longer appearing to resemble the dead woman, he was beginning to feel at one with the city once more. He felt it most keenly on his monotonous interminable walks through the empty streets.

For he was finding it impossible now to remain at home, discomforted in the solitude of his house, with the wind moaning in the chimneys and memories multiplying around him like so many staring eyes. He was out virtually the entire day, aimless, distraught, confused about Jane and his true feelings for her.

Did he really love her? And what indifference or betrayal might she have in store for him? Staggering incertitude! The sadness in those ever-shortening winter afternoons! The floating mists that always spread! He could feel in turn the contagious mist enter his soul, and all those faded thoughts drown in a gray lethargy.

Ah! Bruges in winter, in the evening!

The city's influence was acting upon him again: a lesson in silence from the motionless canals, their calmness worthy of the presence of the noble swans; an example of resignation exhibited by the dark quays; but above all the strict and pious counsel descending from the highest belfries of Notre Dame and Saint-Sauveur, always visible in the background. Instinctively he raised his eyes to them as if searching for sanctuary; but the towers poured scorn on his wretched affair. They seemed to be saying: "Look at us! We are nothing but Faith! Cheerless, without the smiles of sculpture and with the look of airborne citadels, we climb toward God. We are the military belfries. And the Devil has spent his arrows on us!"

Oh, yes! How Hugues would have liked to be as them. Nothing more than a tower, far above life! But unlike the Bruges towers, he could not take pride in having frustrated the intrigues of the Devil. On the contrary, townsfolk claimed this intrusive passion which commanded him was surely an act of possession by the Devil himself!

Stories and accounts of Satanism now returned to him. Could there be some crumb of truth in these fears of occult powers and bewitchment?

And was it not the conclusion of some pact that calls for blood the way this drama was unfolding? At such moments Hugues sensed the shade of death drawing ever closer to him.

He had wanted to elude, conquer, scorn Death through the specious artifice of a resemblance. Maybe now Death would wreak its revenge.

But he could still escape and be exorcised in time! And across those quarters of the great mystic city where he wandered, he raised his eyes once more to the merciful towers, the consolation of the bells, the compassionate embrace of the Madonnas who on every street corner tender their arms from within a niche set among candles and roses covered by a globe, like dead flowers inside a coffin of glass.

Yes, he would cast off this wretched yoke and repent. He had been the UNFROCKED OF SORROW. But he would do penance. He would become again what he once was. Already he was beginning to identify with the city itself, recasting himself as brother in silence and melancholy to this sorrowful Bruges, *soror dolorosa*. Oh, how wise it had been to settle here at the time of his great mourning! Silent analogies! Reciprocal penetration of soul and objects! We enter them while they in turn are absorbed by us.

And so, cities possess above all else a personality, an autonomous spirit, an almost externalized character which corresponds to joy or new love, to renunciation, to bereavement. Every city is a state of the soul, and one hardly need stay there long before this state communicates itself, spreads into us like a fluid which infects, and which one incorporates with the nuances of the air.

From the beginning Hugues had sensed this pale and soothing influence of Bruges and with it he had resigned himself to lonely reflection, the abeyance of all hope, in attendance of a merciful death . . .

And even now in the evening, despite the present anguish, he could yet feel his pain ebb a little in the still waters of the lengthening canals, and he strove to redefine himself once more in the image of the city.

XI

Above all, the City has a Believer's face. Counsels of faith and renunciation emanate from it, from the walls of its convents and hospices, from the numerous churches kneeling in their skirts of stone. Once again, it began to take control of Hugues and inspire his submission. It was becoming an Individual, the principal interlocutor of his life, impressing upon him, dissuading, commanding, to the extent that it influences one's entire orientation and reasons for action.

Hugues soon found himself conquered by this mystic side of the City, now that he was beginning to extricate himself from the figure of sex and deceit of Woman. He paid less heed to such things and was thus more open to the sound of the bells.

Numberless and untiring were those bells, as Hugues in one of his relapses into sorrow would set out at dusk, to wander directionless along the quays.

It felt like a sickness, the tolling of those eternal bells—the obit, the requiem; call to matins and vespers—all day long rocking their dark censers, which one never sees, and from which swells a smoke of sounds.

Ah! Those never silent bells of Bruges, that great service for the dead whose psalmody fills the air! How it spelt out a repugnance of life, a lucid sense of the vanity in everything and a clear signal of death's stealthy approach . . .

In the empty streets where now and then a streetlamp struggled gamely on, rare silhouettes spread apart, common women of the town in their long woolen cloaks, dark as bells of bronze and swaying just like them. And together the bells and cloaks seemed to be heading along the same route to the churches.

Hugues experienced the vague sense of an admonition. He followed them in their wake. He was reanimated by the enclosing ardor. The propaganda of example, the latent will of things was drawing him back to that reverence for the old churches.

As before, he developed a penchant for visiting them toward evening, above all the aisles of Saint-Sauveur with their long black marble expanses, the vainglorious rood-loft from which at times a shimmering music unfurls . . .

This music was a mighty force that streamed down the pipes to the flagstones; and which they said drowned and obliterated the dusty inscriptions on the tomb slabs

and brasses with which the basilica is liberally sown. Here, one could truly be said to be walking amidst death!

And so, none of it, neither the gardens of stained glass, nor the sublime, timeless paintings of Pourbus, Van Orley, Erasme Quellyn, De Crayer, and Seghers, garlanded with tulips that never fade—none could dilute the sepulchral sadness of this place. And even in the triptychs and altar screens, Hugues could scarcely contemplate the feast of color and that eternal dream of distant painters, without musing with even greater melancholy on death, and on the panels, he saw the donor with clasped hands and his spouse with those cornelian eyes—of whom nothing remains but these portraits! And so, he stirred death once more—he had no wish to linger over the living woman, that salacious Jane whose image he left behind at the church door—it was the dead woman he dreamed of kneeling with before God, like those donors of the not-so-distant past.

During his bouts of mysticism, Hugues still loved to go and immerse himself in the silence of the little Jerusalem chapel. It was to here at sunset that the cloaked women would make their way . . . He followed after them; the aisles were low; a sort of crypt. In the far corner of this chapel, erected in adoration of the savior's wounds, lay a life-size figure of Christ in the tomb, livid beneath a fine lace shroud. The cloaked women lit tiny candles, then retreated with sighing steps. And the candles bled a little. In that shadow it was if they were the wounds of Christ himself, reopening, beginning to flow again, to wash away the evils of all who came there.

But, among his pilgrimages through the town, Hugues above all adored L'hôpital Saint-Jean, where the sublime Memling lived and left behind a clutch of guileless masterpieces to express over long centuries the fresh vibrancy of his dreams when quartered there as a convalescent. Hugues also went there in the hope of recovery, to soothe his feverish retina in the lotion of its white walls. That great Catechism of Calm!

The interior gardens, fringed with box, and beyond the sick rooms where voices are hushed. A few nuns pass by, barely disturbing the silence, like the swans of the canals who barely ruffle the waters. An odor of damp linen lingers in the air, of rain-faded coifs and altar cloths just drawn out from antique wardrobes.

Finally, Hugues arrived at the sanctuary of art where those unique paintings dwell, where the renowned shrine of Saint Ursula gleams, like a miniature gothic chapel in gold, unfolding on each side, over three panels, the legend of the eleven thousand Virgins; while in the enameled metal of the roof in tiny delicate medallions one sees the Angel minstrels, with violins the color of their hair and harps in the form of their wings.

Thus, the martyrdom is accompanied by a painted music. It is infinitely gentle this death of the Virgins, grouped together like a mass of azaleas in the moored

galley which is to be their tomb. The soldiers are on the shore. They have already begun the massacre; Ursula and her companions have disembarked. The blood flows, but so pink! The wounds are petals ... the blood does not drip; it sheds petals upon their breasts.

The Virgins are content and perfectly calm, glimpsing their courage in the gleaming mirror of the soldier's armor. And even the bow that delivers death seems somehow softened like the waxing of the moon!

With these delicate subtleties, the artist discloses that the agony in store for the faithful Virgins was merely a transubstantiation, a challenge gladly accepted with the promise of imminent rapture. And this is why the peace which already reigns within them has spread out into the landscape, as if radiating out from their very souls.

A transitory moment: less the carnage than already the apotheosis; the droplets of blood are beginning to congeal into rubies for eternal diadems; and above a drenched earth heaven opens, her light is visible and takes over ...

Angelic appreciation of martyrdom! Paradisiacal vision of a painter both pious and a genius.

Hugues was deeply moved. He dreamed of the faith of these great Flemish masters who passed on to us these truly votive pictures: those who painted as they prayed!

And so it is with all such marvels: the works of art, the silver and gold, the architecture, the houses with the air of cloisters, gables in the shape of miters, streets adorned with Madonnas, the wind filled with the voice of the bells, all surged toward Hugues as examples of piety and sobriety, the contagion of a hardened Catholicism in the air and in the stones.

At the same time the exceptional piety of his early childhood returned to him, and with it a nostalgia for lost innocence. He felt a measure of guilt before God as he did before his wife. The notion of sin was reemerging.

Especially following one particular Sunday evening when by chance he had entered the cathedral for the service and the organ music and was thus present at the close of the sermon.

The priest preached on death. And what other subject to choose in this mournful city where it brazenly flaunts itself and sends its vine of black grapes entwining around the pulpit, right to the very hand of the preacher who has only to pluck them. What to speak of other than that which is omnipresent in the atmosphere: inevitable death! And what other thought to ponder than that of one's soul and its redemption, which is the overriding concern here and the perpetual goad of consciences.

Now the priest expounded on death, the Good Death that was merely a passage and on the reunion of souls redeemed in God. He spoke also of that most treacherous sin, the *mortal* sin, that which makes death

the true death, without deliverance or the recovery of loved ones.

Hugues was listening, and not without a little emotion, behind a pillar. The great church was somber, barely lit by a few lamps and a scattering of candles. The faithful were gathered in a dark mass, almost merging into shadow. It seemed to him as if he were quite alone, that the priest were directly facing him, addressing him personally. By a quirk of fate or the influence of his imagination it was as if the words were relevant to his circumstance. But of course, he was in a state of mortal sin! He had tried to deceive himself over his guilty love and invoke the justification of resemblance. He was an accomplice of the flesh. He was doing exactly what the church most roundly condemned: he was living a kind of concubinage.

Now, if Religion speaks the truth, if saved Christians do rediscover one another, he would never see her again, she the saintly and the painfully missed, for not having desired her exclusively. Death would only eternalize the absence, consecrate a separation he had imagined only temporary.

Afterward, as now, he would live far from her; and his unceasing torment would be to ever remember her in vain.

Hugues left the church profoundly troubled. And from that day the idea of sin obsessed his mind and drove its nail deep. He would so like to be released from it, to be absolved. Perhaps a confession would somehow check the disorientation, the foundering of the soul into which he was sliding. But he had to repent, change his mode of living; and despite the grievances and daily misery, he did not yet have the strength to leave Jane and return to a solitary life.

The City however, with its Believer's face, reproached and insisted, offering the model of its own chastity and strictness of faith . . .

And the bells connived in all this, as now each evening he wandered in growing anguish, with the agony of loving Jane, the yearning for the dead woman, his fear of sin and possible damnation . . . At first the bells argued their sound advice in friendly tones; but soon they lacked compassion and chided him—all around him visible and palpable, like the crows around the towers—harrying him, invading his mind, molesting him to savagely purge him of his forlorn love and tear out his sin!

~~~~~~~~~~~~~~~

　　　　　　　　　　　　　　　RODENBACH

XII

Hugues was suffering; day by day the dissimilarities were more evident. Even the illusion of physical appearance could no longer be sustained. Jane's face had assumed a certain hardness, as well as an air of fatigue, lines beneath the eyes which cast a shadow over that same mother of pearl and pupils of jet. She had also resumed the fancy from her theater days of softening her cheeks with powder, of applying carmine to her lips and darkening her eyebrows.

In vain had Hugues tried to dissuade her from using this makeup, so out of keeping with the chaste and natural face he remembered. Jane scoffed; she was ironical, brittle, irascible. He would call to mind the gentleness of the dead woman, her good humor, her words of such tender noblesse, dropping like petals from her lips. Ten years together without a quarrel, not one of those dark words that rise from the stirred-up depths of the soul.

The difference between the two women deepened every day. But, no! She was never like that! This confirmation pained him, signaling the end of the excuse for an adventure in which he began to see only misery. A mortification, almost a shame overcame him: he no longer dared to dream of her over whom he had shed so many tears and about whom he was beginning to feel guilty.

Rarely now did he enter the rooms eternalized by her memory. He stood distressed, confused in the gaze of those portraits, a look one might have said of reproach. And the tress of hair continued to rest in the glass case, all but abandoned, where the dust accumulated its layer of gray ash.

More than ever, he felt his soul grown weak and crippled: going out, returning, going out again, hounded, one could say, from his own home to Jane's, drawn to her face when he was at a distance and plagued by regrets, remorse, and self-loathing when he found himself beside her.

His household was in a state of disarray too; all punctuality and order had fallen by the wayside. He gave commands, then promptly changed them, cancelling his meals. Old Barbe no longer knew how to organize shopping and housework. Saddened, concerned, knowing well the cause, she prayed to God for her master . . .

Often bills and invoices would arrive demanding large sums for purchases made by that woman. Barbe, who received them in her master's absence, was aghast: a never-ending stream of clothes, trinkets, expensive jewelry, all sorts of objects obtained on credit, using and abusing her lover's name, in the shops of the town where she purchased things incessantly, with a prodigality which mocked expense.

Hugues gave into her every caprice and yet she showed not the slightest gratitude. More and more she indulged in her outings, sometimes gone for a whole day and the evening too, putting off her rendezvous with Hugues, dashing off a scribbled note.

Now she claimed to have acquired a scattering of relations. She had companions. Was she always to live alone? On another occasion, she declared her sister in Lille was sick, a sister she had never mentioned before. She absolutely had to go and visit her. She was away several days. On her return the same games started up all over again: the chaotic life of absences, departures, back and forth, like a fan, flux and reflux where Hugues's life was suspended.

Eventually, his suspicions were aroused; he would spy on her and prowl about her house of an evening, nocturnal phantom of a slumbering Bruges. He knew well the secret look-out place, the breathless halts, the sudden ringing of the doorbell whose sound quickly fades down passageways which guard their silence, the keeping watch outside until late into the night before a lit window, the screen of a blind upon which a shadow-play silhouette passes, and one imagines at every moment to see another.

He didn't even concern himself with the dead woman anymore; it was Jane whose charm had relentlessly bewitched him and whom he feared losing now. It was not only her face but her flesh, her whole body whose blazing vision was evoked from the far side of night and whose hovering shadow he made out there in the very folds of the drapes ... Yes! He loved her, because he was consumed by jealousy to the point of affliction and weeping, when through the long evenings he kept a close watch on her, scourged by the carillon of midnight, by that incessant light rain of the North, where without letting up the clouds fray into drizzle.

And he remained, lying ever in wait, passing back and forth in the cramped space of a courtyard, muttering aloud indistinct words like a sleepwalker, despite the rain that grew heavier: slush, mud, and cloudy skies, the close of winter, all the wretched sadness of things ...

How he would have liked to know, elucidate, see ... Oh, the torment! What kind of soul did this woman possess to wound him so, while the other, the one so pure—the dead woman—seemed in these supreme moments of his distress to rise up in the night and regard him with the pitying eyes of the moon.

Hugues was no fool: he had cottoned on to Jane's lying and worked the rest out for himself; and soon he was even more aware of the facts when, as is the custom in these provincial cities, letters arrived, anonymous cards brimming with sarcasm and invective, sordid details of the deceits, the licentiousness he had already suspected ... Names, all the evidence were supplied. So here was the conclusion to his cheap liaison; a cause so worthy at first had now led him astray. As for Jane, he would be done with her; that much was clear! But how to rectify the degradation within himself, the grief, now that he was the object of ridicule and the sacred shrine to his beloved, that most heartfelt despair, was now the focus of public derision?

Hugues was distraught. Jane too was over for him; it was if the dead woman had died a second time. Oh, all he had endured from that conniving capricious woman!

One last evening he went to say his farewells, determined to rid himself of the onerous burden of sorrow weighing on his soul which she had inflicted.

Calmly and with immeasurable melancholy, he recounted all he had learned; and since she responded negatively, with disdain and a flourish of bravado: "What? What on earth are you talking about?" he presented her the shameful incriminating papers ...

"Are you really gullible enough to be taken in by anonymous letters?" And she let out a cruel laughter, exposing her ivory teeth, teeth designed for prey.

Hugues remarked: "Your little games had already enlightened me."

Jane, in a sudden rage, came and went in a slamming of doors and a swishing of her skirts.

"So! What if it is true?" She retorted.

Then, a moment later:

"And anyway, I've had enough of living here! I'm leaving."

Hugues had observed her while she was speaking. In the lamp's brightness he saw again her clear face, the black pupils, her hair of dyed gold, as false as her heart and her love! No! Her face was no longer that of the dead woman; but she, trembling in that robe with her throat throbbing, was certainly the woman he had embraced; and on hearing her cry "I'm leaving," his entire soul toppled inward, turning to face an eternity of darkness . . .

In that solemn moment, he felt that apart from the illusion of resemblance, he had also loved her in sensorial terms—a belated passion, a sad October inflamed by the chance of a late flowering rose!

All these notions whirled around in his head: He knew only one thing, he suffered abominably, he was sick, and he would no longer suffer if Jane did not threaten to leave. Even now he still desired her. Inwardly he was ashamed of his cowardice; but he couldn't go on without her . . . Besides, who knows? The world is so cruel! She had not even bothered to justify herself.

Then, suddenly, he was struck by a monstrous anguish at the end of this dream whose agony he had endured (the ruptures of love are not unlike death, in that there are always departures without farewells). But it was not only the separation from Jane nor the cracks in the mirror of reflections which aggrieved him at that moment: he sensed the looming threat of a return to loneliness—face to face with the city—with no one between them. For sure, he had made the choice, this irremediable Bruges and its gray melancholy. But the burden of shadow from the towers was too heavy. And Jane had made him feel that shadow fairly reaching across his soul. Now he would give in to it all. He would be alone again and pray to the bells! Even more alone, as if widowed for second time! And the city too would seem even more dead than before.

Hugues, distraught, leapt toward Jane, clasped her hand and implored: "Stay! Stay! I must have been out of my mind . . . ," his voice limp, moistened by tears, as if he had wept inside himself.

That evening, walking home along the quays, he felt troubled, fearful of some as yet unknown danger. Gloomy thoughts assailed him. The dead woman haunted him. She seemed to return, hovering in the distance, wrapped in a shroud, adrift in the fog. Hugues judged himself even more guilty in her regard. Suddenly the wind stirred. The poplars edging the canal whispered in lament. Some disturbance on the canal unsettled the swans, those beautiful secular swans, a century old, expiatory swans, who, according to legend, the City was bound to care for in perpetuity, having unjustly put to death a lord who had worn them on his coat of arms.

Now the swans, ordinarily so calm and white, took fright, ruffling the silken shimmering waters of the canal, skittish, restless, moving around one of their number who beat his wings and then, leaning on the others, rose from the water, like an invalid stirring, trying to leave the sickbed.

The bird seemed to be suffering: at intervals it cried out; then with a last effort raised itself into flight, the cry grew more distant and softened; a wounded voice, almost human, inflecting like a melody . . .

Hugues watched and listened, bewildered by this mysterious scene. He recollected the popular belief. Yes! The swan really was singing! For it was approaching death or at least sensed it in the air!

Hugues shivered. Could it be meant for him, this ill omen? The ugly scene with Jane, her threat to leave, had set him up only too well for these dark forebodings. How would it all end for him? For what fresh mourning were these crepes of the superstitious night? Of what will he be the widower of now?

XIII

Jane took full advantage of this moment of alarm. With her flair for being an adventuress she had realized that day what power she exercised over this man so consumed by her and malleable to her will.

With a handful of words, she had completely reassured him, reconquered him, installed herself untainted before his eyes, enthroned herself once more. Then she had reckoned that at his age, strained by prolonged grief and sick as he was, so changed already over these last months, Hugues would not last much longer. Now, he was known to be wealthy; one of the town's more reclusive inhabitants and a stranger to most. It would be folly on her part to let such a legacy slip through the net when it could be so easily secured!

Jane toned down her behavior, reduced her outings to those that seemed plausible, and took greater care in venturing anywhere deemed risky.

One day she was taken with the idea of visiting Hugues's house, that vast ancient mansion on the Quai du Rosaire with its air of opulence, impenetrable lace curtains, that tattooing of frost on the panes, permitting no passing gaze to determine what lay beyond.

Jane would have relished crossing the threshold, speculate on his fortune through his displayed wealth, inspect his furnishings, his jewelry and silverware, all that she coveted in order to make a mental inventory of everything she had resolved to appropriate.

But Hugues had never agreed to receive her there.

Jane resorted to her sly ways. It was as if their relationship were reborn, a warm and pleasant honeymoon period. The perfect moment now presented itself: it was May; the following Monday was the procession of the Holy Blood, a centuries-old annual Cortege to the shrine where a drop of Christ's blood from the Wound made by the spear is conserved.

The procession would pass along the Quai du Rosaire right beneath Hugues's windows. Jane had never witnessed the procession and expressed curiosity. It would not be passing her own house, which was too far away; and it was unlikely she would get to see any of it in the overcrowded streets, since on that day, people descend from all over Flanders.

"So, what do you say? I'll come to you . . . we'll dine together . . ."

Hugues countered that the neighbors and servants would only gossip.

"I'll come early, when everyone is still asleep."

He worried also about Barbe, so prudish and devout, who would take her for an envoy of the devil.

But Jane insisted: "So then! We're agreed?"

And her voice was cajoling; that voice from the first days, a voice of temptation that all women manage at certain times, a crystal voice which sings, widens to a halo, into eddies where men surrender, whirl around, and lose themselves utterly.

~~~~~~~~~~~

XIV

That Monday Barbe rose very early, earlier than she was used to, for she had only a part of the morning to pre-pare the decorations on the house before the passing of the procession.

She attended the early Mass at five-thirty, took communion with a measure of fervor, then, on her re-turn, began the preparations. The silver candelabra were brought out from the cupboards, as were little ruby vases and burners for incense. Barbe rubbed and polished each object until they gleamed like mirrors. She also took out delicate cloths to lay on the small tables she placed be-fore each window, a temporary repository, a charming altar dedicated to the month of May and to Mary, with candles enclosing a crucifix and a statuette of the Virgin herself...

There were also the external decorations to con-sider, as on this special day everyone competed in pious zeal. According to custom, the facades had already been adorned with the green and bronze pine boughs that the peasants carried from door to door, and which formed along the streets a double row of trees, like a hedge.

From the balcony Barbe hung clothes in the papal colors, white fabrics in chaste folds. Enthusiastic, nimble, fully occupied, she bustled to and fro, handling with veneration this annual decorative ritual which for her amounted to a cult of worship, as if the priests' very fingers, imbued with holy oils, had consecrated all with an inalienable blessed water. She felt as if she herself were in a sacristy.

It only remained for her to fill the baskets with herbs and cut flowers: that fleeting mosaic, a scattered carpet with which each servant colors the front of their house at the moment the procession passes. Barbe hurried on, slightly intoxicated from the scent given off by the hollyhocks, giant lilies, daisies, sage, rosemary, and reeds which she cut into short ribbons. And her hand plunged into the basket, rejuvenated by this massacre of corollas, fresh cotton wadding, the quilts of dead wings . . .

Through the open windows came the building concert of the parish bells sounding one after another.

The weather was gray, one of those undecided days in May when despite the clouds, there is a kind of after-joy in the sky. And owing to this delicacy in the air, where one guessed each fresh peal of bells, a certain gaiety spread from them to her; and the ancient bells, the worn-out ones, old grandmothers on crutches, those of

the convents and the old towers, those stay-at-homes, valetudinarians who guard their silence all year only to emerge and take their places on the day of the Holy Blood—all seemed beneath their worn bronze skirts to wear a cheerful white surplice, crimped undergarments in fan-like folds. Barbe listened to the chimes, the mighty cathedral bell heard only on special holidays, slow and dark, striking the silence like a crook . . . and all the little bells from neighboring turrets, all excited, jubilant in their silver gowns as if forming their very own procession across the heavens . . .

Barbe's piety was enthused; that morning it seemed as if a real fervor was in the air, that some ecstasy was shedding its petals from the skies with the pealing of those bells, and one heard the invisible wings of angels passing.

And everything seemed to converge on her soul, where she felt the presence of Jesus, where the host whom she had embraced at the dawn Mass was now radiating out, still whole, a perfect sphere in whose center she made out a face.

The old servant, ever dreaming of the goodness of Jesus, he who was truly within, crossed herself and resumed praying, the taste of the Blessed Sacraments lingering on her lips.

But her master had summoned her; it was his lunchtime. He took the opportunity to inform her that he was expecting a guest for dinner and that she should make all the necessary arrangements.

Barbe was taken aback; he had never received anyone! It all seemed most odd; then suddenly a dread thought entered her mind: suppose what she previously feared was now about to happen, that which having been somewhat reassured, she had driven from her thoughts—but she had guessed it, yes, of course! It was that woman, the one Sister Rosalie had talked about, could it be she who was coming? . . .

Barbe felt her blood run cold . . . If so, she had made up her mind, her duty was clear: to welcome that creature, serve her at table, obey her orders, associate herself with such sinfulness, no, this had been expressly forbidden by her confessor. And today of all days! A day where the very blood of Christ would pass before the house! And she, who had received communion that very morning! . . . But no! It could never be! She would have to take leave of his service at once.

She had to know, and with that touch of tyranny which comes easily to the servants of elderly bachelors or widowers in the provinces, she enquired:

"Whom will Monsieur be receiving as dinner guest?"

Hugues replied that it was a little bold to ask him such a thing and that she would know soon enough when the guest arrived.

But Barbe, overcome by a suspicion which seemed more and more plausible, and seized by fear and now a real sense of panic, decided to risk everything so as not to be caught off guard and she replied:

"Is it not a lady that Monsieur is expecting?"

"Barbe!" retorted Hugues, regarding her in a surprised and rather severe manner.

But she didn't relent:

"I need to know in advance. Because if Monsieur is expecting a lady, I must inform him that I will be unable to serve at dinner."

Hugues was bewildered: was he dreaming? Had she lost her mind?

But Barbe firmly repeated that she was going to leave; she could not continue; she had already been forewarned; her confessor had commanded her to depart. She was not about to disobey, clearly, and place herself in a state of mortal sin, to die a sudden death and descend to Hell.

At first Hugues understood none of it; but gradually he untangled the shadowy web, the likely gossip, the rumored adventure. So, now even Barbe knew? And she was threatening to leave because Jane was coming? Then wasn't that woman to be derided, if his humble servant, bound to him for so many years by habit, by the thousand threads that each day unwind and spin themselves between two complementary existences, preferred to break and quit rather than serve her just once?

Hugues was exhausted, dazed, his uplifted mood crushed before this sudden unforeseen crisis which was ruining his happy plan for the day, and with an air of resignation he simply stated:

"Barbe, you may leave immediately."

The old servant reflected and suddenly, good common soul that she was, filled with pity, realizing how he suffered, shook her head, and in a soft singing voice which Nature had bestowed on her for lulling babes to sleep, she murmured:

"Oh! Jesus! My poor Monsieur! ... And for such a woman, a very bad, bad woman ... who deceives you ..."

And for a moment, forgetting the social distance, she had become maternal, ennobled by divine pity, her cry gushing forth as from a spring which bathes the wound and can heal ...

But Hugues silenced her, vexed and humiliated by this meddling, by her audacity in speaking of Jane and in such terms! It was he who was giving her notice and right away! She could come the following day and collect her belongings. But she must leave today, at once!

Her master's annoyance removed any last scruples Barbe might have had in leaving so abruptly. She put on her fine black hooded cloak, content in herself and in this sacrifice to her moral duty, and to Jesus who reigned within her ...

Then calmly and without emotion, she left that house in which she had lived for the past five years: but before setting off she cast about her in front of the building the contents of the baskets she had emptied into her apron, so that the street, if only at this spot, was not without its carpet of corollas beneath the feet of the procession.

XV

How badly the day had begun! One would think all cheerful plans are a challenge! Overlong in preparation they allow ample time for fate to switch the eggs in the nest and we are left to brood on sorrows.

Hugues, hearing the door of the house slam shut after Barbe, experienced a dreadful sensation. Another problem, a deeper solitude, since the old servant had been part of his life. All this was down to Jane, that cruel and capricious woman. How much he had already suffered in her name!

How he wished she wouldn't come. He felt morose, troubled, on edge. He pondered the dead woman ... How had he come to believe the lie of that resemblance, so quickly seen to be flawed? And beyond the grave, what must she think of the arrival of another in a home still so much her own, sitting in the armchairs where she had sat, superimposed in the line of mirrors where the countenance of the dead endures, the newcomer's face over her own?

The bell rang. Hugues was obliged to open the door himself. It was Jane, late and flushed from her brisk walk. Brusque, imperious, she entered, taking in with a single glance the great hallway, the rooms with their open doors. Already one could hear the echo of distant music growing nearer. Before long the procession would be here.

Hugues had lit the candles on the window ledges himself and on the little tables which Barbe had arranged earlier.

He went upstairs with Jane to his room on the second floor. The casement windows were fastened. Jane went to open one.

"No!" said Hugues.

"But why?"

He explained to her that she could not let herself be seen and would attract attention to the house. Especially during the passing of the procession. The provinces are prudish. They would soon be talking of a scandal.

Jane had removed her hat in front of the mirror; powdered her face a little with the puff from a small ivory box she always had with her.

Then she returned to the window, her hair uncovered and lustrous, that copper gleam drawing the eye.

The crowd thronging the street looked up with curiosity at this extraordinary woman with her vivid hair and clothing.

Hugues's patience was exhausted. One could see enough from behind the drapes. He leapt forward and slammed the window shut.

Jane took offence, lost interest in watching further and slumped on the sofa with a steely and unyielding air.

The sound of the procession welled up. You could tell it was drawing closer by the widening ripples of the canticles. Deeply pained, Hugues turned away from Jane, resting his feverish brow on the glass pane, a freshness of water that helped dissolve the anguish.

The first children from the choir were passing by: singers with short, cropped hair, chanting and bearing candles.

Hugues could make out the procession clearly through the windows, in which certain characters stood out like those painted gowns in the background of religious images fashioned in lace.

Members of the congregation passed by bearing pedestals with statues, sacred hearts; holding banners of hardened gold aloft like stained glass; then groups of the innocent, the verger in white robes, the archipelago of muslin from which incense unfurled in tiny waves of blue—the council of virgin children around the paschal lamb, white like them as if made from curls of snow.

Hugues turned an instant toward Jane who, still sulking, remained sunk in the sofa, appearing to brood on the darkest thoughts.

Now the music of the serpents and Ophicleides rose more solemnly to bear that more delicate and intermittent garland, the soprano.

And through the window Hugues saw before him the knights of the Holy Land, the Crusaders, swathed in gold and armor, the princesses of Bruges legend, all those related to Thierry d'Alsace who brought the Holy Blood back from Jerusalem. Now it was the young who filled these roles, the sons and daughters of the most noble aristocracy of Flanders, dressed in ancient cloth, rare lace, and precious family jewels. It seemed as if all those saints, warriors, and donors of Van Eyck's and Memling's paintings were suddenly made flesh, restored to life by some miracle from their eternal resting place in the museums.

Hugues could barely watch, so overwhelmed was he by Jane's irritation, and so incredibly sad, even sadder during these canticles which pained him so. He tried to pacify her. At his first utterance her mood was one of defiance.

And she turned to face him, bristling, like hands filled with things with which to wound him ever more deeply.

Hugues, silent and dejected, turned in on himself, launching his soul, so to speak, into the swelling music that whirled along the streets, so it might sweep him far away from his self.

Next came the clergy, monks of every denomination advanced: Dominicans, Redemptorists, Franciscans, Carmelites; then the Seminarists in pleated tunics, reading their antiphonaries; then priests of every parish in their red chorister attire: vicars, curates, canons, in chasubles and embroidered dalmatics, glinting like gardens of precious gems.

One could discern the clinking of censers. Bluish smoke billowed in wreathes all around; each little bell united in an ever more sonorous hail that resonated in the air.

The bishop in his miter appeared beneath a canopy, bearing the shrine of a miniature cathedral in gold surmounted by a cupola where, amidst a thousand cameos, diamonds, emeralds, amethysts, enamels, topaz, and delicate pearls, dreams the sole ruby possessed of the Holy Blood.

Hugues, seduced by this mystical aura, by the fervor of all those faces, the faith of this vast crowd thronging the streets under his windows, as far as the eye could see, to the very ends of the city at prayer, also bowed his head when he saw at the approach of the Reliquary everyone sink to their knees, yielding to the flurry of the canticles announcing its approach.

Hugues had almost forgotten the reality of the situation, Jane's presence, the latest scene which had just formed an ice field between them. Seeing his tender emotion, she sniggered.

He made as if he hadn't noticed, suppressing surges of hatred for this woman which were now intermittently flaring up inside him.

Haughty, icy, she put her hat back on, as if she were preparing to leave. Hugues dared not break the ominous silence which now lay over the room in the aftermath of the procession. The street had quickly emptied yet belied that overwhelming sorrow which settles after a joy has passed.

She went downstairs without a word, but there, appearing to have second thoughts or else seized by insatiable curiosity, she looked back from the threshold at the rooms with their doors left invitingly open. She took a few steps and quickly slipped into those two vast adjoining rooms, the severity of whose bearing seemed to condemn her. Rooms too possess a physiognomy, a face. Between them and us lie friendships and immediate animosities. Jane felt unwelcome, awkward, and out of place, unnerved by the mirrors, hostile to the time-worn furnishings whose unchanging attitude seemed threatened by her very presence.

Lacking discretion, she pored over everything ... she noticed portraits here and there, on the walls and pedestal tables; they were the pastels and photographs of the dead woman.

"Ah, so this is where you keep your portraits of women?" And she laughed with a hint of malice.

She moved on to the hearth:

"Look at this one! She even looks a little like me . . ."

And she picked up one of the portraits.

Hugues had been observing her moving around with great agitation and now suddenly felt a deep wounding at this unwittingly cruel joke, this vile jesting which chafed against the saintliness of the dead woman.

"Leave it be!" he said in an imperious manner.

Failing to understand, Jane burst out laughing.

Hugues advanced, took the portrait from her hands, shocked by the contact of these profane fingers on his memories. He always handled them with trembling awe, as if they were sacred objects, like a priest handling the monstrance and chalice. His grief had become a religion. And in that moment, the candles, not yet extinguished, which had been burning on the ledges for the procession, lit up the rooms as if they were chapels.

Jane, sarcastic, took a perverse delight in Hugues's distraught bearing, and secretly wishing to undermine him even more, she swept into the next room, touching everything, upsetting the trinkets, creasing the fabrics. Suddenly she stopped and let out a resounding laugh.

She had noticed the precious glass case on the piano and out of bravado lifted the lid and took out the long tress of hair. Astonished and amused she let it unravel and waved it in the air.

Hugues had turned ashen. This was profanation, the final sacrilege . . . For years now he had not dared touch the divine object which belonged to death. And now that whole cult of the relic, with so many tears stippling the crystal each day, had ended up a mere plaything for the woman who mocked it ... Oh how long now she had caused him suffering! All his rancor, the waves of suffering drunk, sieved through every second, every minute of the hour of each month, the suspicions, the betrayals, the waiting beneath her windows in the rain: all of it surged over him at once ... Now finally he would chase her out!

But as he sprang forward, Jane, in defiance, sought refuge behind the table, acting as if it were all a game, dangling the tress at a distance, lowering it toward her face and mouth like some charmed serpent, coiling it around her neck, the feather boa of a golden bird ...

Hugues cried out, "Give it to me! Give it to me!"

Jane ran left, then right, whirling around the table.

In the frenzy of the chase and goaded by her laughter and sarcastic asides, he lost his head. He caught hold of her. She still had the tress around her neck and struggled, not wanting to give it up, furious now and cursing him for hurting her with the tight grip of his fingers.

"You won't?"

"No!" she said, still laughing nervously beneath his grip.

Then Hugues lost himself entirely; a flame sang in his ears; blood burned in his eyes; a dizziness raced through his head, a sudden frenzy, a tightening of the fingertips, a desire to seize, to wring something, to break flowers, his hands now had the strength of a vice—he had seized the tress still wound round Jane's neck; he must have it back! And frantic, unyielding, he pulled on it wildly until fully stretched it was tight as a cord around her neck.

Jane no longer laughed. She let out a faint cry, a sigh, like the breath of a bubble expiring on the waters' surface. Strangled, she collapsed.

. . . .

She was dead—for not having guessed the Mystery and the presence of that which must not be touched on pain of sacrilege. She had lain her hand on the vengeful tress, that hair which as an emblem—for those whose soul is pure and communes with the Mystery—meant that at the moment it was profaned it would itself become the *instrument of death*.

And thus, the whole house had died: Barbe had gone, Jane was no more, the dead woman was in death even more dead than ever . . .

As for Hugues, he looked without comprehending, knowing nothing anymore . . .

The two women had been as one. So alike in life, still more so in death which had bestowed upon them the

same pallor, he could no longer tell one from the other—
the unique face of his love. Jane's corpse was the ghost of
the former dead woman, visible there now to him alone.

Hugues, his soul regressing, could only recall the
most distant things, the beginning of his bereavement,
to which he believed he had now returned ... Quite
calm, he seated himself in an armchair.

The windows were still open ...

And in the silence came the sound of bells, all of
them at once, ringing again for the return of the procession to the chapel of the Holy Blood. That splendid
cortege was over ... all that had been, had sung out, offered life, the resurrection of a morning. The streets were
empty again. The city prepared to be solitary once more.

And Hugues went on repeating: "Morte ... Morte
... Bruges-la-Morte ..." in a mechanical voice, a calm
voice, seeking to harmonize: "Morte ... Morte ... Bruges-la-Morte ..." with the cadence of the last bells: le-
thargic, slow, weary little old women who seemed—was
it over the city, over a tomb?—to be languidly shedding
flowers of iron!

Will Stone is a poet, essayist, and literary translator. His first poetry collection, *Glaciation* (2007), won the international Glen Dimplex Award for poetry in 2008. His subsequent collections, *Drawing in Ash* (2011), *The Sleepwalkers* (2016), and *The Slowing Ride* (2020), were critically appraised. Will's published translations from French and German include the collection *Poems* by Georges Rodenbach (2016) as well as works by Georg Trakl, Stefan Zweig, Joseph Roth, Georg Simmel, Maurice Betz, Rainer Maria Rilke, Gérard de Nerval, and Emile Verhaeren. Recent published translations include *Poems to Night* by Rilke (2020), *Encounters and Destinies: A Farewell to Europe*, by Zweig (2020), and *Nietzsche in Italy,* by Guy de Pourtalès (2022). Will has contributed to a number of publications including the *Times Literary Supplement*, *Apollo Magazine*, the *Spectator*, *RA Magazine*, *Irish Pages*, *Modern Poetry in Translation*, the *Bitter Oleander*, the *London Magazine*, and *Poetry Review.*

IMAGING ARCHITECTURE